Also by
Carlton Mellick III

Satan Burger
Electric Jesus Corpse (Fan Club Exclusive)
Sunset With a Beard (stories)
Razor Wire Pubic Hair
Teeth and Tongue Landscape
The Steel Breakfast Era
The Baby Jesus Butt Plug
Fishy-fleshed
The Menstruating Mall
Ocean of Lard (with Kevin L. Donihe)
Punk Land
Sex and Death in Television Town
Sea of the Patchwork Cats
The Haunted Vagina
Cancer-cute (Fan Club Exclusive)
War Slut
Sausagey Santa
Ugly Heaven
Adolf in Wonderland
Ultra Fuckers
Cybernetrix
The Egg Man
Apeshit
The Faggiest Vampire
The Cannibals of Candyland
Warrior Wolf Women of the Wasteland
The Kobold Wizard's Dildo of Enlightenment +2
Zombies and Shit

PARASITE
MILK

CARLTON MELLICK III

ERASERHEAD PRESS
PORTLAND, OREGON

ERASERHEAD PRESS
205 NE BRYANT
PORTLAND, OR 97211

WWW.ERASERHEADPRESS.COM

ISBN: 978-1-62105-249-4

AUTHOR'S NOTE

I didn't feel like writing a real introduction to this book, so here is a recipe for spaghetti tacos:

SPAGHETTI TACOS

INGREDIENTS:

Leftover spaghetti
Taco shells
Frozen meatballs
1/2 cup canned diced jalapenos
2 1/3 cups shredded Mexican blend cheese
1 tablespoon cayenne pepper
1/4 cup chili paste
Two large eggs
1 bottle of vodka
Some nails
A really cool custom-made post-apocalypse motorcycle
    from the Mad Max movies
A shotgun
Your face
Robot arms (optional)
Cilantro

Place the leftover spaghetti in a large mixing bowl and stir in the eggs, cayenne pepper, diced jalapenos, and chili paste. If you don't have any hands use robot arms (optional). Put mixture in medium casserole dish, insert frozen meatballs, and cover with Mexican blend cheese.

Heat casserole in the oven for 45 minutes at 350 degrees.

While baking, drink the entire bottle of vodka and hammer the nails into your face, then drive the motorcycle around the block, firing the shotgun wildly into the air. This should encourage your neighbors to form a post-apocalypse biker gang with you. Lead your new friends back to your place for lunch.

Put the spaghetti mixture into taco shells and garnish with cilantro. If any of your new friends has that weird genetic disorder that makes cilantro taste like soap, tell him to get the fuck out of your house and never come back. You don't need to associate with *their* kind.

This recipe should make two dozen tacos. Share with your friends. Or eat all of them while they watch in order to establish your dominance as leader of the biker gang.

Enjoy!

Or if you're really lazy you could just toss a can of Chef Boyardee into a taco or whatever. I don't care.

So that's it. I hope you enjoy my new book.

—Carlton Mellick III 6/10/2017 8:58pm

CHAPTER
ONE

I have way too many erections.

Seriously, I have a ton of them. At least twenty a day. Fifty, sometimes, if the weather is warm enough. It's a curse. A horrible, never-ending curse. When I was a teenager, they said it was normal. They said all boys are plagued by frequent erections from the time they go through puberty until the time they reach their sexual peak. They said it would all calm down some time during college. But they were wrong. They were completely, utterly wrong.

After all the other boys in my class passed their sexual prime, my libido kept on growing. It only got stronger as I aged. By the time I was thirty, the problem was three times as bad as it was when I was a teenager, dealing with erections on an hourly basis. Now I'm almost forty and it's even worse. It seems like I spend most of my day erect and painfully horny. The doctors don't know what to make of me. They just give me pills that are designed to calm my sexual urges, but nothing ever seems to be strong enough to nullify them completely. I still suffer from constant, unending erections that seem to come out of nowhere. In the most unlikely of places. At the most awkward of times.

Right now, for instance.

I'm on a crowded teleportation pod, six dozen passengers squeezed together as tightly as Vienna sausages in a can, waiting to be beamed halfway across the galaxy to the planet Kynaria. Just as they locked the doors and I found myself pressed against the back of an eighty-year-old frog woman, my penis decided to grow hard. It's poking into her like a child poking his finger into a frosted birthday cake, and there's absolutely nothing I can do about it.

I attempt to think of the most sexually unappealing things I can possibly imagine. A fat man naked? No. My grandparents having sex? No. Making out with the old lady in front of me? Definitely no. I can't think of sex. No matter how disgusting in concept, any thought of sex will keep me aroused. I try thinking of something mundane. I think of math. I do math problems in my head. But my erection won't go away. Thinking of math just reminds me of my high school algebra teacher—Mrs. Davila, the hot twenty-three-year-old who wore low-cut shirts for absolutely no reason other than to torture fourteen-year-old boys.

The old frog woman won't sit still, wheezing and shifting her weight from side-to-side, unintentionally rubbing her shiny, warted skin against my dick. I'm not sure which planet she is from. I'm hoping it's one of the more open-minded worlds that have come to accept that erections are perfectly normal bodily functions that are in no way offensive or embarrassing. Or better yet, perhaps she comes from a planet where they don't have erections at all and don't even know what they are, like the Tryxians who mate by blowing bubbles at each other from tubes in their armpits.

I decide to think of something frightening. The best way to get rid of an erection is through anxiety. It should be easy. I'm standing in a teleportation pod, waiting to be dematerialized and instantaneously beamed thousands of light years away from Earth. That's already a pretty scary idea. And a whole lot of things can go wrong.

Traveling via teleportation beam is supposed to be perfectly safe, but there are instances of people being sent to the wrong planet or disappearing into the great void of space. There's also a chance that you'll become particle-locked, where you come out on the other side as an unmoving statue of flesh. Or you can become beam-resistant, where your anatomy can no longer safely dematerialize and you'll be forever trapped on the planet you've just visited, which may not be your home world or even a habitable world at all.

The possibilities are all very frightening. However, they do nothing to kill my erection. The idea of being trapped on an alien planet is almost comforting to me. At least I'd never have to worry about my embarrassing erections ever again.

"You the eyebot man?" somebody asks me.

I peer over the woman's shoulder and see a large guy with a thin gray beard squeezing through the crowded teleportation pod toward me. He's one of the only humans in the chamber besides me. He pushes past a blue blobby creature and elbows a young stick-thin elf woman in the neck, raising his eyebrows with a big smile on his face as though excited to make my acquaintance.

"Eyebot man?" I ask him, not quite sure he's talking to me.

He nods. "Don't you run the eyebots? You know, the camera drones? I was told that the eyebot guy would be taking the beam with me."

I'd never heard of the term *eyebot* before. I wonder if he came up with the nickname himself.

"Yeah," I say. "Do you work for the show, too?"

He holds out his hand and introduces himself. "Mick Meyers."

I know the name. He's one of the producers on the show. After I shake his hand, he wipes his fingers down the gray whiskers on his chin as though using my palm sweat for hair gel.

"Irving Rice," I say.

My erection does not dissipate, even after shaking the guy's hand. For a second, I'm almost happy to be pressed against the old woman so that my penis is concealed from his view. But then she moves. Mick shoves her out of the way so that he can stand in front of me. My only choice is to cover myself with my hands as the crowd squeezes us into each other.

"Nice to meet you, Rice," Mick says.

He smiles down on me as though he can tell I've got my dick in my hand, but he doesn't acknowledge it. He just stands in silence, pressed against me with that awkward smile on his face. I try not to look him in the eyes.

After a few unbearable moments, he breaks the silence by asking, "So, have you ever been to Kynaria before?"

I shake my head. "I've never even been off world at all."

His eyes light up. "So this is your first beam? How exciting for you. You must be thrilled."

I shrug. The idea of teleporting to an alien world always kind of frightened me.

"Yeah, I guess."

"The first beam I took was to Chung. Have you heard of Chung?"

I shake my head.

He says, "Chung is a fire planet. It's all lava and the people there have rock-like skin. It's crazy."

Ever since Earth was connected to the intergalactic transport system, we've had access to thousands of alien worlds. So many that I haven't even heard of the vast majority of them. I didn't even know about the planet Kynaria until a few weeks ago, when I was told they needed me to go there for a shoot.

"The girls there are really hot," Mick continues. "Even though the outer layer of their skin is made of stone, they still have amazing curves and perfect tits. They're like marble statues that walk and talk. If you ever have a chance to have sex with a Chungian, I highly recommend it." He chuckles and rests his hand on my shoulder. "And man, they give the most amazing blowjobs."

Mick raises his voice as he talks about the Chungian women, as though he wants to make sure that everyone in the chamber can hear what he's saying. Many eyes, both alien and human, turn toward us.

He continues. "You see, even though their skin is hard as rock on the outside, inside they are really soft. Their mouths and tongues are just heavenly goo."

Mick's words don't help my erection at all. And with his hand on my shoulder, the situation couldn't possibly get more awkward.

"But they're nothing compared to the women on Oolva," he says. "I'm sure you've heard of Oolva. The really curvy tall girls with the purple tentacles? They have these giant lower mouths big enough to swallow a man whole. When they give you a blowjob, that's what it feels like. Everything from your waist down goes in their mouths. It's something you've got to try."

I'm beginning to think Mick is a very strange individual. He's only just met me, yet he's already telling me the kinds of things you'd only tell your closest friends in a private setting after you've had a few too many beers. Listing your favorite alien blowjobs is not the kind of anecdote you tell to a guy you just met, especially not on a crowded teleportation pod.

"But make sure you only do oral with an Oolvan," he continues. "Their vaginal fluids are like acid. They'll melt your dick right off. Seriously. A friend of mine learned that the hard way. He hasn't fucked anything since."

He laughs and grips my shoulder tighter.

"But the weirdest blowjob I ever got was—"

He is cut off by a voice coming on the intercom system telling us that we will depart in ten seconds. The lights dim. The room begins to vibrate.

"Here we go," Mick says, finally removing his hand from my shoulder. "Get ready to have your molecules dispersed."

He smiles as though excited by the idea of dematerializing, like it gives him some kind of physical thrill.

When the countdown reaches zero, my skin becomes warm with vibrations. It feels like we're being cooked inside of a microwave. Then I lose my senses one at a time. First, the sense of sound. Everything goes silent as my ears come apart. Then goes my sight. Everything becomes fuzzy and pixilated, then black. My sense of touch lingers much longer, but all I feel is the warm vibration of my skin as it is broken down into particles.

The only sense that I don't seem to lose is my sense of smell. Perhaps it's just my brain messing with me, but I can't get the scent of burnt rubber out of my nose. It sticks with me even after I become a bodiless mass of information projected across the galaxy.

When I am put back together, I realize that my erection

has finally subsided. Who knew that all it took to end my humiliation was for me to have my entire body broken down on a molecular level and sent to another world?

"Here we are," Mick says, rubbing his beard. "This is going to be fun."

I nod my head. But I'm not sure if I agree. I didn't come to have fun. I'm just here to do a job. If I were the adventurous type I would have traveled to another world long ago.

The overhead lights brighten and the doors to the chamber open.

As we wait for the people ahead of us to leave the pod, Mick says, "Kynaria is one of the most beautiful worlds I've ever been to. It's a mushroom planet. There's no trees here. No wood. Everything's made of mushroom."

I nod. It's all I really know about the planet. There's not a whole lot of information about Kynaria online. All I know is that it's really colorful and mushrooms grow like crazy.

"You've been here before?" I ask.

He nods. "I came last month to scout locations. It's a pretty crazy place. You're going to love it."

"When does Andrew come?" I ask.

"In a few days. We've got a lot of work to do before then, but there should be time to see the sights and have a little fun."

He winks at me as he says *a little fun*. I really don't want to know what he means by that.

"Who else is already here?" I ask.

He looks at me as though he has no idea what I'm

talking about.

"Who else?" he asks.

"The crew," I say. "Is anyone going to meet us?"

Mick shakes his head. "The crew? What are you talking about? *We're* the crew."

"I mean the rest of the crew."

"There is no rest of the crew. You're doing the filming. Andrew will be in front of the camera. I handle the rest. We'll have a guide or two, but it's basically just us."

"Are you serious?" I ask.

He pats me on the back. "No big deal. We can handle it."

"How come they only sent two people? They sent ten times as many for the Byron One episode."

He shrugs. "It's Kynaria. Nobody wanted to go to Kynaria. You have to have guts to come to a backwards planet like this one."

Just before we exit the teleportation pod, Mick smiles at me. "That must have been why they sent the two of us. We've got more guts than any of them combined."

The transport station doesn't look any different than the one back on Earth. The same building materials, the same architecture, the same bland gray colors. There just aren't too many humans in sight. In fact, besides Mick, myself, and a few Japanese business men exiting our teleportation pod, there aren't any other humans in sight. The place is full of beings from hundreds of different planets across the galaxy, each one more surreal than the last. I don't recognize a single one of them. Some of them are small and furry. Others are the size of elephants with multiple small human-like limbs. There's a red snake-like man slithering toward the baggage claim. A feathered one-eyed lady with webbed feet and a long black beak sits in the food court, regurgitating bugs into her children's mouths. There were plenty of these visitors at the transport station back on Earth, but it seems stranger when experiencing it as one of the aliens, rather than one of the natives.

Mick smiles at the expression on my face as he catches me alien-watching.

"Pretty fascinating, aren't they?" Mick asks, licking his lips as he admires a three-breasted kangaroo-like woman with pink fur strutting across our path.

"Which ones are the Kynarians?" I ask.

I'd seen a picture of one online before my trip, but none of these people look anything like that one did.

"Most of them are Kynarians," he says. "Can't you tell?"

He points out the Kynarians. They are the large blob-like ogres that fill the station. At first, I didn't realize they were all the same species. They come in so many different colors and shapes. They range from deep emerald green to bright fluorescent pink to blue and yellow striped. Though some of them are fat and blob-like, others are tall and thin. The only thing they have in common is that they all seem mushroom-like, with large bell-shaped heads. I'm not sure if they evolved from mushrooms or if they just evolved to blend in with their mushroom surroundings, but they definitely look like the kind of beings that would live in a world dominated by fungus.

As I get close to one of the Kynarians, a strong pungent truffle-like odor fills my nostrils. It's so offensive that I have to step back and cover my nose.

Mick looks at me, wondering what's wrong.

"It smells in here," I say.

He nods in agreement, but doesn't bother to cover his nose. "Yeah, every planet has its own unique funk that you have to deal with. The smell is everywhere. You'll get used to it."

I shake my head. I have no idea how I'll get used to this kind of stench.

After we get our luggage, we leave the transport station and head into the alien city.

"Look at that, Rice," Mick says, standing on the sidewalk with his arms outstretched. "This is what you were missing staying on Earth all this time."

The sky is pink and blue and purple, covered in large billowing clouds that are deep red in color as though they're filled with blood instead of water. The buildings are built into the sides of massive golden mushrooms larger than any skyscraper back on Earth. The streets are paved with smooth blue glass and instead of vehicles, people ride on the backs of giant slugs that move faster than any car I've ever seen.

The sight is overwhelming. I've seen pictures of alien worlds, but nothing prepared me for actually being on one. I need to sit down to catch my breath, only there's nothing recognizable as a chair for me to sit down on.

"Come on," Mick says, patting me on the back so hard I nearly fall over. "Let's check into the hotel and then go get a beer."

"They have beer here?"

He shrugs. "Well, the Kynarian equivalent to a beer."

I agree, but I am not too sure about the idea of drinking strange alien alcohol, or even getting drunk on an alien planet. But Mick doesn't seem like the kind of guy who takes no for an answer. And since he has nobody else to drink with, I don't think there's any chance he'd let me talk my way out of it.

CHAPTER
TWO

We take a slug taxi across town. It's all automated. No need for a driver. The slug is supposed to be telepathic and knows where you want to go without you having to say so. It's very convenient. Still, riding on the back of a slug isn't something I expected to be doing on my trip. You're able to sit inside of an enormous cushy seat designed to fit the largest of Kynarians, but there's no floor between your feet and the slug. Mick rests his shoes right on the slimy back of the creature, dipping his toes in gray ooze. But I can't get myself to do that. I just hold them up in the air for the whole ride.

When we pull up alongside the entrance to a large mushroom hotel, I think the slug must have brought us to the wrong location. This isn't at all where we were supposed to go.

"We're here," Mick says.

I shake my head, not wanting to leave the taxi.

"I thought we were going to stay in a human hotel," I say. "That's what they told me."

Mick frowns. "Hell no. That shithole is in Earthtown.

There's no way we're staying in Earthtown. Where's the fun in that? I cancelled our reservation and got us a place here. You don't go to Kynaria without living like the Kynarians."

"But…"

He doesn't let me say another word. He pulls me out of my seat and waves the giant slug away.

"You'll love it," he says. "Trust me."

The second we get into the Kynarian hotel room, I realize I should never trust Mick to make decisions for me ever again.

"I don't love it," I tell him. "I don't love it at all."

"Are you kidding me?" Mick says. "This place is amazing."

I look at him and then back at the hotel room. There aren't any beds in the room, at least nothing I'd recognize as a bed. The majority of the floor is taken up by a large pool of black mud.

"Are we supposed to sleep in that?" I ask, pointing at the mud puddle.

He nods. "That's how the Kynarians sleep."

"In mud?"

He nods again. "Sure, why not? They say it's warm and soothing. It's supposed to be good for the skin."

"Human skin or Kynarian skin?"

He shrugs. "I'm sure it's perfectly safe for human skin."

I examine the mud more closely. It's bubbling like a tar pit. I couldn't imagine how you'd be able to sleep in there.

"Do we sleep naked in that thing?"

"Yeah."

"And we sleep in it together?"

"Kynarians always sleep in groups, so yeah. Don't worry though. We can sleep on opposite sides. It's not gay or anything."

"And we won't drown?"

"Probably not."

"And what do we use for pillows?"

He points at the cushioned rim of the pool. "You sleep with your head out of the mud. It's not all that soft, but will support your neck okay."

"But we'll wake up every day covered in mud…"

"It's fine. They probably have a shower or something in the bathroom."

"Are you sure?" I ask.

He shrugs. "Check it out."

I cross the room, careful not to slip and fall into the mud. The bathroom doesn't look anything like the bathrooms on Earth. For one thing, there's nothing that resembles a toilet, a sink, or a tub. There is a large basin in the center of the floor made from what looks to be a bear-sized clamshell. A constant stream of water pours into the shell like a waterfall.

"Is this it?" I ask.

Mick comes over and nods his head.

"Yeah, that's it."

"What about the toilet?"

He looks away and scratches the back of his neck. "About that…"

I look at him. "What?"

"A Kynarian shower kind of doubles as the toilet."

I look at the shower and then back at Mick. "Huh?"

"Kynarians don't have anuses. They defecate through their skin, so they don't have any use for toilets."

"So they shit in the shower instead?"

"Yeah…"

"So we have to shit in the shower as well?"

He rubs his beard at me. "To tell you the truth, it's not entirely unpleasant."

"Are you serious?"

He shrugs. "You'll get used to it." Then he turns to the bathroom closet and opens its doors. "It's really not that bad. It's just a pain because you have to undress and dry off every time you want to take a dump." He puts his hand under the stream of water. "At least the water's warm."

After we unpack our clothes in the bathroom closet, Mick takes me out for dinner and drinks.

"Since we're going to be living together for a couple of weeks, we should get to know each other a little better," he says.

We don't wander too far from the hotel. Mick takes

us to a place just down the street. It's not a typical tourist spot. It's a real Kynarian restaurant that caters only to Kynarian clientele. We're the only two offworlders in the place.

"If you're in Kynaria, you have to eat authentic Kynarian food," Mick says.

He sits us down at a table right in the center of the place, like he wants everyone to notice that we're here.

"Is Kynarian food any good?" I ask.

Mick shrugs. "I don't know. Not really. But it's still the right thing to do."

I nod my head.

"They have a McDonald's over in Earthtown now," he says. "Could you imagine that? Coming all the way across the galaxy and eating at McDonald's? It's blasphemy."

I nod my head.

Mick continues, "We've only been a part of the teleportation network for five years and there's already a McDonald's on every fucking planet in the galaxy. Can you believe that shit? It makes me embarrassed to be human."

He pauses to think about it for a moment. And then, in a slightly ashamed tone, he says, "Although I guess I've been to all of them. I'm always tempted to try the unique alien menu items…"

Before we get any menus or order any food, a small toadstool of a waitress comes by and puts plates on our table. Then she delivers two fizzy drinks.

"What's this?" I ask. "Did they give us somebody else's food?"

Mick shakes his head. "Nah. This is how they do it at restaurants in Kynaria."

He picks up a pink chunk of food from his plate and stuffs it into his mouth.

Between chews, he says, "You don't get to choose what you eat like you do on Earth. Kynarian restaurants serve you whatever they want to serve you. They see you as a guest in their home. When you go to a dinner party, you don't demand your hosts make you whatever you want them to make you. You have to eat what you're given. That's what it's like on Kynaria. Actually, that's what it's like in restaurants on most worlds I've been to. Earth restaurants are actually pretty unique in that way."

I nod and look down at my plate. I've been given something different than Mick. The stuff on the right of my plate looks a bit like blue sauerkraut, while the left half of my plate contains a slab of mystery meat in some kind of yellow gravy.

I don't know if I'm happy or worried that I've been served food that I didn't order myself. On one hand, I probably wouldn't have been able to understand the menu or known what I was ordering anyway. On the other hand, I could have been given anything. This blue sauerkraut could be some kind of slug-like creature's pubic hair for all I know.

"Don't think too much about it," Mick says. "Just eat it. You're better off not knowing."

There aren't any utensils resembling forks or spoons. Mick just eats with his hands, so I decide to follow suit.

"The Kynarians have long hooked fingernails they

use to eat with, so they don't need forks or chopsticks or anything."

I nod my head and pick up a pinch of the blue sauerkraut stuff. When I put it in my mouth, the flavor overwhelms me. It tastes kind of like rotten peaches soaked in gasoline. I swallow it anyway.

"Is this stuff safe for human consumption?" I ask.

"Most of it is," he says.

Saliva pools in my mouth.

"What do you mean *most* of it?"

"Well, they have a lot of mushroom-based foods here. And you know how there's a lot of poisonous mushrooms back on earth? Well, there's even more poisonous mushrooms here. And Kynarians are resistant to most forms of mushroom poison so they sometimes put them in their dishes."

As he talks, saliva has pooled so much inside of my mouth that it spills over my lips and down my chin.

"But don't worry," he says. "I researched it thoroughly and would recognize any of the poisonous dishes they serve."

I hold my hand over my face, but the saliva keeps on coming.

"Are you okay?" Mick asks, finally noticing that something is wrong with me.

"My salivary glands are going nuts." The flow of fluid becomes so bad I can hardly speak. "I'm drooling all over the place."

He nods his head. "Yeah, you must be having some kind of allergic reaction."

"Allergic reaction?" I gurgle.

"Yeah, you probably shouldn't be eating that. It's probably not safe."

"Not safe?"

"Just eat the yellow stuff. I've had that before. It's grub steak. It won't hurt you."

Saliva drenches my shirt. "Grub steak?"

"Never eat blue stuff on an alien world," he says. "No good ever comes from eating blue stuff."

It takes a while, but eventually my drooling calms down. I eat the grub steak, pretending that it didn't come from a worm the size of a cow, and take sips of the fizzy beverage until my saliva glands return to normal. The only thing that actually tastes good is the beverage. It is sweet, but not offensively sweet. It reminds me of what a dandelion soda would taste like if I ever drank a dandelion soda. It's not until I'm halfway through the beverage that I realize it's highly alcoholic.

"It's actually frog semen," Mick says.

I have no idea what he's talking about until he points at my beverage. "You're drinking fermented semen."

I look down at my white drink.

"You're fucking with me…" I say.

He laughs and shakes his head. "No, seriously. There's this amphibious frog-like animal that produces a sweet semen that the Kynarians use to flavor all sorts of desserts and alcoholic drinks."

"Are you kidding me?" I ask. "That's disgusting."

"No, it's delicious," he says.

He takes a long gulp of his fizzy frog semen.

"You should put this on the show," I say.

"What? The frog semen drink?"

I nod my head. "It's perfect."

"Nah," he says. "Andrew won't do any alcoholic beverages. Maybe we can have him try one of the frog semen desserts, but not this drink."

"Why won't he do alcoholic beverages?"

"He doesn't drink. He'll talk about bizarre alcoholic beverages on the show, but he won't drink them."

"So do you already know what weird foods you're going to have Andrew eat?"

"I've got plenty of leads, but we need to nail them all down before he gets here later in the week."

"What's the grossest food you've got lined up so far?" I ask. "Anything worse than frog semen?"

"A *lot* worse," he says. "The frog semen is actually delicious. I could drink it every day. The viewers at home will think it's disgusting, but that's because they only imagine it would be terrible to drink." He takes another sip. "The *really* disgusting dish involves anal shellfish."

"Anal shellfish?" I ask.

"Yeah," he says. A smile creeps onto his face. "On Kynaria, there aren't any oceans or large bodies of water, so they don't have seafood like we do. But there's a lot of different species of parasitic crustaceans and mollusks that they eat instead. For instance, the Kynarian version

29

of lobster is a three-pound parasite that they harvest from the bellies of large mammals. The Kynarian version of a crab is this foot-long spider-like bug that infests the feathers of birds like lice or fleas. But anal shellfish... Man, anal shellfish freak the hell out of me..."

He pauses to take another bite of his food.

As he chews, he says, "There are a lot of large animals on Kynaria. Some of them are as big as dinosaurs. But there's this one creature that is far bigger than anything else on this world. It's like a woolly mammoth, but ten times the size of a brontosaurus. Anyway, this beast produces many species of parasites the locals consider to be the ultimate in fine dining. One of them is what I like to call anal shellfish. There are these large clams that grow inside the anus of this dinosaur creature, huge clusters of clams the size of my fist. And they smell absolutely horrible, even when cooked. I can only describe it as rotten fish mixed with stomach flu diarrhea."

I cringe. "And you're going to have Andrew eat it?"

He nods. "And not only that, but we're going to have him climb into the creature's ass and harvest them himself. It's going to be great television. I bet it will be one of the best episodes of *Bizarre Foods* yet."

"Do you think he'll really go through with it?"

"Of course. He's Andrew Zimmern. He'll eat anything."

"How is he able to do it anyway?" I ask.

"Who?" Mick asks.

"Andrew Zimmern. How is he able to eat all those weird alien foods? I wouldn't be able to do it. I'd puke all over the place."

"You don't know?" Mick asks.

I shrug.

Mick explains, "Andrew used to be a heroin addict. For about a year, he was homeless and eating out of dumpsters. He grew a tolerance for eating disgusting food. I guess once you've lived off of rotten meat and molded bread for long enough, you come to appreciate all kinds of foods, even stuff the average person wouldn't be able to stomach."

"I didn't know he was a heroin addict."

"Well, he's not anymore. He's been sober for years. That's why he won't drink alcohol or do substances of any kind. He really turned his life around. Going from a junkie in the gutter to a world-famous celebrity, the man is an inspiration. A hero for recovering addicts."

I nod my head, finding a new admiration for the star of the show I work on.

Then Mick chugs his drink as the waitress brings him two more.

After dinner and a few more drinks, we take a drunken stroll through the Kynarian city, following the road of slug-vehicles, admiring the iridescent lights that radiate from the giant mushrooms around us. The place is even more beautiful at night. Everything glitters with blue and green light. There are three moons in the sky, one of them so big and bright and red that it could be its own sun. Glowing butterflies the size of eagles flutter overhead, shimmering like fireflies, filling the night like stars.

The air is also thick with spores. White fluffy mushroom dust floats down on us like snowflakes, covering the city in powder. The smell is pungent and earthy. When I inhale the spores, my throat becomes itchy and raw. It's becoming difficult to breathe.

"Is this stuff toxic?" I ask Mick, as I cough on the descending spore cloud.

He shrugs. "I was here for two weeks and never had any problems."

"It's hard to breathe," I say.

I also realize that my skin itches and my eyes are watering.

"It's probably just this planet's version of allergies," he says. "Did you have bad seasonal allergies back home?"

I nod at him, keeping my nose and mouth covered.

"Then maybe we should get you some antihistamines. I'm sure they have some in Earthtown."

"You think that would be enough?" I say through my fingers.

He nods. "Of course. Allergies are the same on every planet."

As we walk down the sidewalk, an alien woman grabs our attention. She's not wearing any clothing and looks like no woman I've ever seen before. She has large gemstone eyes and her blood glows with blue light, radiating beneath her paper white skin. Her hair is energy, like purple fire. And her flesh is as smooth as jellyfish skin.

Just one look at her and I find myself becoming erect. When she passes, Mick turns around to get a look at her back. He licks his crusty lips and doesn't remove his eyes from her for a second.

"Oh, man..." he says, moaning with lust. "I love alien women that don't bother with clothing. Makes it so much easier to size up the goods."

"What planet is she from?" I ask.

Even though I constantly try to avoid ogling sexually attractive women in public, I can't stop myself.

"Manticore," he says. "I've never been there but it's definitely on my bucket list."

The woman looks back at us, noticing we are staring at her. I doubt she can speak English, but it definitely seems like she knows we're talking about her.

As I divert my eyes, Mick says, "Don't look away. In their culture, it's rude *not* to admire their bodies in public."

"Are you serious?" I ask.

The woman gawks at us with her gemstone eyes. Her face is expressionless. I can't tell if she's annoyed or pleased with our behavior.

My penis becomes more erect as she looks at me. It's even worse than it was back at the transport station. I'm not sure, but it feels as though her species has this effect on males.

When the woman turns back and walks away, Mick groans and kicks the glassy sidewalk.

"Damn it, she's not into us," Mick says.

"How do you know?" I say.

"In Manticore culture, it's proper etiquette for males to stare down females they're attracted to. If the females share the attraction, they let you know immediately, usually by grabbing your dick and pulling you back to their home. If they're not interested they'll just look you up and down, then move on."

"So why is it rude to *not* admire their bodies in public?" I ask.

"Huh?" he asks, still staring at the woman as she walks away from us.

"You said not to look away from her," I explain. "Why would that be rude?"

Mick snaps out of it as the woman turns a corner.

"Oh, it's basically like calling them ugly," he says.

I nod, then cover my erection with my hand.

When I look down, I notice Mick has just as big of an erection as I do. Only he doesn't try covering it up. He sees me looking at his dick. Then looks at mine, then looks at his, then we have the most awkward moment of silence I've experienced in my life.

Mick laughs and points at my dick. "You must be thinking what I'm thinking!"

I have no idea what he's thinking and I really don't know if I want to find out.

"We need to get laid!" he says.

He pats me on the back and waves down a slug-taxi.

"Let's hit up a whorehouse," he says. "I've been dying to hit up a Kynarian whorehouse all week."

The idea of going to a whorehouse turns me off. I even lose my erection a little.

I shake my head and hold out my hands. "No, it's okay. I think I'll just go back to the hotel room."

He points at my dick again. "Not with *that* boner you're not. You need to relieve that tension. It's unhealthy to ignore it."

A slug-taxi pulls up next to us on the side of the road, waiting for us to board. Its massive blubbery flesh pulses and oozes at me, strangely bringing my erection back up to full standing.

"I'm fine, really," I say, my face growing red with embarrassment. "This is nothing."

He shakes his head. "I don't see it going away. You're going to have to come with me. I insist."

"Do you even know where to find a brothel?"

"No, but the taxi will find it for us. The thing is telepathic. It will know exactly where we want to go."

Before I can think of a good enough excuse, I find myself crawling up onto the slug's back with Mick. Then we take off. A part of me is worried. I've never even wanted to go to a brothel on Earth, let alone one on an alien planet. And Kynarians are ugly and smell bad. I have absolutely no desire to have sex with one.

CHAPTER
THREE

"This is going to be fun," Mick says along the way. "My favorite part of visiting alien worlds is sleeping with the native women."

I nod, but do not agree with his words one bit. I'm not at all excited about going to an alien brothel. I'm terrified.

"Are they safe?" I ask him. "What about sexually transmitted diseases?"

Just the thought of what kind of crazy STDs exist on Kynaria sends me into a panic.

He frowns at me and waves my words away. "Don't be such a wimp. Just wear a condom."

"But didn't you just tell me earlier today that you had a friend whose dick melted off by having sex with an Oolvan woman?"

"Yeah, but there probably won't be any Oolvan women. It's a Kynarian brothel."

"Well, what if Kynarians have weird penis-melting diseases you don't know about yet?"

"Look, I've slept with dozens of aliens on dozens of

different worlds and never once have I gotten anything more than a cold. All you need is a condom and you'll be fine."

I stare out the window, watching the mushroom buildings pass us by. I don't bother arguing with Mick anymore. There's nothing he can say that will ease my worries.

Mick says, "If you want to play it safe, just get a blowjob. You're always safe with a blowjob."

The cab leaves the city and takes us deep into the mushroom forest. There aren't any buildings or lights out here. We're riding the only slug on the road.

"Where are we going?" I ask, trepidation rising in my voice.

Mick stares out the window. His voice expresses just as much panic as mine, but he doesn't show it.

"The place must be out of town," he says. "It's okay, though. All the best stuff is off the beaten path."

"Do you think it got our destination wrong?"

It's a terrifying thought to be at the mercy of a telepathic slug. It could take us out into the middle of nowhere and die. It could think we wanted to go to a city on the other side of the planet.

"No, I'm sure it's taking us to the right place. These slugs have always been accurate every time I've ridden them in the past."

"So you're not worried?"

He rubs his gray whiskers and shakes his head. "No, of course I'm not worried."

But he looks obviously worried.

An hour of back roads and trails of unpaved soil that slows the slug-taxi down to a third of its speed, and Mick finally admits he's worried.

"The Kynarian wilds aren't anything to fuck with," he says. "We definitely don't want to get stranded out here. They've got spiders that can eat a horse."

I look out the window and see nothing but mushrooms and packs of wild snails out there.

"How do we get this thing to turn around?" I ask.

He shrugs. "You just think about wanting it to turn around and it turns around."

"So should we think about turning around?"

But just as I ask the question, lights appear up ahead. We pull up alongside a mushroom house that is much smaller than those in the city but still enormous by Earth standards. It looks kind of like the Kynarian equivalent to a roadhouse bar.

Mick wipes his brow with relief and says, "We made it. We actually made it."

We jump out of our seats into the thick soil and take a few steps toward the door, stretching our legs and backs. The front of the building is filled with half a dozen slug vehicles that slither around each other, waiting for their riders to get back.

"This place looks perfect," he says, breathing the fungal smells into his nose.

I look back to see the slug-taxi slithering off, leaving a slime trail in its wake. Part of me wants to jump back on the thing and return to the city. But even at a third of its speed, the slug moves far too quickly for me to catch up.

After it's gone, I look back at Mick and ask, "Is that thing coming back to pick us up later?"

Mick shrugs. "We'll worry about that after we're done."

I translate this to mean: "If we have to stay here all night, I'm perfectly fine with that."

The inside of the brothel is quiet, like a library. Old, blobby Kynarian men sit at a bar, drinking sludgy brews. They don't look at each other or say anything. They just drink and stare. I wonder if this actually is a brothel at all.

"I don't see any women," I tell Mick.

He looks around the room and nods his head. "They've got to be somewhere."

We see a shriveled toadstool man enter from the back room and step behind the bar, wearing what appears to be a burlap sack with holes cut into it.

"I'll go figure it out," he says.

Then he leaves me standing by the entrance with the old mushroom men glaring at me. I wonder if this place was a brothel at one time, but is now some kind of drinking hole for the local forest hermits. Or maybe it is a brothel, but they've just got a single prostitute in the back who's so old she looks like a sagging, withered oyster mushroom.

But as Mick attempts communicating with the bartender using an outdated translation device that doesn't seem to be working, I see something out the back window. Three women are outside on the back porch, peeking through the windows at me. They have pink and blue skin with flowing tentacle-like hair and long pointed ears. They don't look anything like the Kynarian women I've seen so far. They are much smaller, at only about five feet in height at the tallest. But they're more attractive and more human than any other creature I've seen on this planet so far, despite their bright colored skin and floppy hair.

I was wrong. There are women here. They must be out on the porch for a smoke break, or whatever the Kynarian equivalent to a smoke break might be. With all the boring disgusting old clientele in the bar, I completely understand why they'd want to hide outside for as long as possible.

One of the women notices me, her red beaming eyes lock on me like she's trying to seduce me. I have no idea if they're actually Kynarian women or women from a different world, but I do know that Kynarians come in all sorts of varieties. This variety could be the one that's actually beautiful. Or perhaps they are considered ugly by Kynarian standards, which is why they have to work in a rundown backwoods brothel like this one.

My erection is back in full force just by making eye contact with the woman outside. I wasn't actually planning on going through with having sex with any of the women at this place, but after seeing her I don't know how I'll be able to resist. Perhaps it's just the fermented frog semen talking, but from this distance she looks prettier than the prettiest girls back on Earth.

"Come on," Mick says to me, snapping his fingers to get my attention. "They're upstairs."

I nod my head and follow him toward the stairwell. Looking back at the window, the women are no longer there. I hope they've gone to meet us on the second floor.

"You're in room two," Mick says, pointing at the door next to his. There are only four rooms, but I would have preferred the one on the other end. Nothing is a bigger turn off than hearing somebody you know having sex on the other side of a wall.

He disappears into the first room and leaves me standing there in the dark mold-scented hall, staring at the faded-orange door. I don't hear anyone on the other side. If it's not the girl with red eyes that I saw outside, I hope the girl is one that is just as attractive. It better not be one of the large blobby toadstool Kynarians I saw in the city.

"Hello?" I say, knocking on the door.

I'm not sure why I speak. It's not like a Kynarian

would understand me.

"I'm coming in…"

The door takes all my strength to open. Since nothing is constructed from wood, it appears to be made of rock and clay, so the door is heavy and difficult to open. Or perhaps it's just heavy for me because humans aren't as big and strong as Kynarian men.

Inside, the room is just a closet and bathroom. I close the door behind me. Standing there in the dark room, lit only by blue glowing worms that wiggle up the walls, I realize this is some kind of changing room. I undress and put my clothes on the shelves. My penis is so hard with anticipation that it pokes into the door as I try to get it open to enter the next room.

"Hello?" I call out again.

The bedroom is similar to our room back at the hotel, only far grungier. It's just a pit of black mud that appears cold and diseased, probably hasn't been changed out in months. Nobody is in here with me—not the girl from outside, not even a blobby toadstool woman. I probably have to wait here until she comes.

There's nowhere to sit, so I just lean my bare butt against the cold mushroom wall, staring into the black muck.

"Shit…" I say, once I realize that I'm going to have to enter the disgusting pool of mud.

I didn't think of that before coming. If Kynarians sleep in the mud they surely fuck in the mud as well. I'm probably supposed to get inside and wait for the woman to come.

"This is a horrible idea…" I say.

But I don't know what else to do. The room is too cold to just wait here naked. The mud will probably give me some kind of warmth. Besides, it's possible the woman won't come unless I'm in the mud and ready to go.

I dip my toe into the black sludge and it cracks apart like the skin on chocolate pudding. But the mud isn't warm at all. It's freezing. There's no way I'm going all the way in.

Something moves within the mud and I pull my toe out. Then a larger blob of flesh explodes from the black pool at me. I fall onto the hard floor and crawl backward. The thing oozes in my direction.

"Are you kidding me?" I cry.

This is the prostitute I'm supposed to sleep with? It's not the girl from outside. It's not a blobby toadstool woman. It's some kind of freakish slug monster.

The thing lunges at me like it's trying to mount me, crawl on me and rape me against the floor. The massive muddy worm opens a slimly hole on its abdomen, aiming it at my erection. But before it can get me, I crawl back into the bathroom and kick the door shut with my foot. The slug slams against the door once, then twice, then it goes quiet. I hear it oozing and pulsing, then sliding back into the muck.

"Fuck this," I say. "I'm out of here.

I put my clothes back on and leave the room. Through

43

the next door, I can hear Mick moaning with pleasure, crying out like he's having the sexual experience of a lifetime. I don't know if he got an actual woman or slug monster, but at least he's enjoying himself. I want to get as far from the place as I possibly can.

Downstairs, I realize that I can't leave. I've got to at least wait for Mick to finish, and that means waiting by myself with a lot of old mushroom men that don't speak my language. I don't have a translation device, so I can't even order a drink. And my erection is still killing me.

I contemplate going back upstairs and hiding in the bathroom, but then I remember the woman who was peering through the window earlier. I wonder if she's still out there. I wonder if she's available. Surely they won't mind if I sleep with her instead of the slug creature upstairs. Unless the slug creature is what you get when you can't afford one of the real women.

I go outside through the back door and step out on the porch, but the women are no longer here. I check around the side of the building. There's no sign of them and there are no other entrances. I peer in the windows, but they aren't inside either. I walk around the outside of the bar, stepping through mushrooms and deep purple soil, but it's like they were never here.

I'm about to give up and go back in when I hear crackling sounds in the forest behind me. I turn and see one of them. The one with the red eyes is standing right behind me, glowing in the moonlight. She had been approaching me while my back was turned. When I see her, I jump and let out a small cry. The pink woman is

44

just as startled as I am and runs away, ducking behind a tree-sized mushroom.

I wonder why she's so afraid. Perhaps she's never seen a human before. Perhaps she's lived in the backwoods her whole life and hasn't seen a whole lot of tourists from other worlds.

"Hello?" I call out. "It's okay. I'm just a customer."

I know the woman can't understand me, but I'm hoping she might at least understand the inflection of what I'm saying.

"I'm a human. From Earth."

The woman peers out from behind the mushroom, appraising me. She doesn't say anything, just stares fixedly with her red beady eyes.

"Do you want to come inside?" I ask.

She doesn't move.

I sigh and look away. I guess she's not interested in me. Perhaps I just look too weird for her.

"I understand," I say. "It's okay. I'll leave you alone."

I turn around and head back toward the entrance. Then there are crackling noises behind me. I look back over my shoulder. The woman is following me, moving slowly and carefully. When our eyes meet, she freezes. She doesn't move. Just stares.

When I turn to face her, she hops two steps back.

Looking at her up close, she is even more beautiful than I realized. She doesn't wear any clothing, like the Manticore woman back in the city. Her skin is brightly colored. Pink face and chest, blue limbs and hair, and her flesh is purple where the colors meet in the middle.

I take a small step forward and she hops back again. When I take a few steps back, she comes forward. It's like we're doing some kind of dance.

"Are you coming or staying?" I ask.

I just stand still, not sure what she wants me to do. She looks down at my erection and up at my eyes. Then slowly, carefully approaches me. As she draws near, I can smell her. She doesn't have the same pungent odor as the city Kynarians. She smells like flowers, like sweet morning daffodils. It's just as strong of a smell, but I like it. It's actually pleasant. She's over ten feet away, but her flowery aroma overwhelms my senses. It clogs my sinuses worse than the mushroom spores that rained onto the city sidewalks.

"You're really pretty," I say.

I don't know why I say it. It's a stupid thing to say, especially when she doesn't know my language. But her fragrance is doing something to me. I'm beginning to feel drunk. Or *drunke*r, I should say.

She comes into the light and I can get a better look at her. Upon closer examination, I don't think she's related to the same Kynarians I saw in the city at all. She must be a different race. Instead of being a mushroom person, she's more of a flower person. Her hair is not made of tentacles, as I first thought, but long blue plants—or something designed to resemble plants, perhaps for camouflage from predators. She also has a long tail that points straight up into the air like that of a velociraptor.

So if she's not a normal Kynarian, what the hell is she? It's like she's some kind of nymph of the mushroom forest. Either way, she's absolutely beautiful. And the more I inhale her scent, the more attracted to her I become.

When she sees me deeply inhale her scent, taking in more of her intoxicating fragrance, she becomes more relaxed and comfortable with me. She seems pleased that I enjoy her aroma. Perhaps for a flower woman, inhaling each other's fragrance is the way you communicate your attraction to each other.

She comes closer and reaches out to me. She goes straight for my penis, rubbing the outside of my pants. Her perfume grows even stronger. I look down on her head, admiring her leaf-like strands of hair. I can see the red roots where the leaves grow into the flesh of her scalp. She slides her small blue hand down the front of my waistband and caresses my erection. Her skin isn't the same as human skin. It feels moist and spongy. I reach out and touch her breast. It's small and unusually firm. It feels like the skin of a dolphin or a string ray. When I rub the left nipple, it swells and leaks a few droplets of white oil, like some kind of natural lubricant.

She pulls away from me and steps back. She runs through the moonlight, disappearing into the mushroom forest.

"Where are you going?" I ask.

She peeks out at me from the shadows.

"You want me to follow you?" I ask.

She just stares at me with her red eyes, looking at me and back at the brothel. It's almost like she's worried somebody might see us. I wonder if she doesn't want to have sex inside. Perhaps these flower women are more like humans and don't like to sleep inside of pools of mud. Perhaps she prefers to have sex in nature, under the stars. It would be just like a forest nymph to desire this.

"Okay, I'll follow," I tell her.

Then I head into the shadows after her.

The mushroom nymph leads me deeper into the forest and I quickly lose track of her. I begin to wonder what the hell I'm doing out here. Mick said they've got giant people-eating spiders out here. It's probably not the kind of place you want to wander around in after dark. But I keep going. I'm too enraptured by her, too drunk on her aroma.

I have to follow her scent in order to find her again. I track her through the mushrooms, through tall blue plants that match the hair that grows on her head. When I see her again, she's lingering in front of a small home. Not exactly a home, more like a nest in the side of a large hollowed-out mushroom stem.

When I come near, she steps out and approaches me. She takes me gently by the hand and pulls me into the mushroom with her, laying me down in a soft bed made of some kind of cotton-like substance. Even though it smells of earthy fungus, the nest is far more comfortable than the mud bath back at the hotel. I could probably sleep here tonight if the woman would let me.

She seals up the entrance to her room by kicking

soil and plants in front of it, basically burying us both alive inside her room. I don't complain about it though. It seems like a weird thing to do, but it's another world. They do things differently here. Perhaps it's for safety, perhaps it's for warmth, or perhaps it's just the traditional way these flower people close their doors.

There's no light inside the fungus room until the woman presses her body against me. Her skin illuminates with my touch. When I rest my hand against her chest and pull it away, a glowing blue handprint remains, as though activated by my body warmth. The light slowly fades, requiring me to touch her again in order to brighten the room, to see her beautiful face.

When I kiss her, she doesn't kiss me back but she doesn't pull away either. It's like she doesn't know what kissing is for, like it's not something they do in her culture. Her breath is sharp and acidic. Her saliva burns my lips. It tastes like I'm kissing an overly ripe kiwi fruit.

The woman pushes my face away from hers so that she can climb on top of me. She claws at my pants, trying to get them off. She must never have encountered a belt or zipper before. I'm not sure if it's because she's not accustomed to clothing or if Kynarians don't use anything like belts or zippers for keeping their clothes up.

I help her undo my pants and she grabs my penis before I can kick them all the way off. I pull off my shirt and pull her close to my body.

Her skin brightens against me, filling the entire mushroom hole. She tightens her legs against my thigh, rubbing her crotch against my knee. As her vagina touches me, her skin glows even brighter. It's as if her iridescence is not caused by my touch, but by her sexual arousal.

The idea sobers me a little. I remember that this isn't a human girl. It is some kind of being from a completely different world, some strange species that evolved in a completely different way than humans have. I wonder how close her DNA is to mine, if it is even compatible. I wonder if we could produce offspring if we decided to mate for real.

A thought flashes into my mind. I didn't bring a condom with me. I didn't think I would actually go through with having sex with an alien prostitute, so I wasn't worried about it. Otherwise, I would have asked Mick for one.

The woman is ready. She doesn't seem to even care about using protection. She straddles me, rolling her purple hips in a circle, trying to maneuver my penis inside of her.

"No…" I tell her, grabbing her by her hips and holding her back. "I'm sorry, but I can't."

Then I remember Mick saying that if I really wanted to be safe, I should stick to getting only blowjobs. So this is what I'm going to have to do. Even though this woman's saliva is acidic and will likely burn my urethra, at least it'll be a lot safer.

I pull myself up and try to move her head down toward my penis, but she resists.

"I can't do that," I say, shaking my head at her. "Only with your mouth."

I point at my mouth.

"Just the mouth."

But she doesn't understand me. I push more firmly on her, but she resists harder. Since she doesn't know anything about kissing, I wonder if she also doesn't know anything about oral sex. I decide not to push the issue. The last thing I'd want to do would be to force her to do something she didn't want to do.

When I release her, she forces all of her weight on me faster than I'm able to escape. I try to wriggle out from under her, but she pushes me hard against the ground. She lays her chest against mine and bites down on my collar bone. Her bite isn't meant to be aggressive or even sexual. It's like she's just trying to hold me down with her teeth.

"Let me up," I tell her, prying her teeth from my neck. "I have to go back."

The second I get her mouth off of me, something sprays in my face. It's the same flowery fragrance she normally emits, only now it's in a wet, concentrated form. It squirts from her armpits, like a skunk spraying from its tail, and hits me like a grenade of tart peach.

Her scent calms me down, makes me want to stop resisting. I wonder if it's some kind of pheromone the flower women use to attract mates, because the smell definitely makes me crave her. It makes me drugged and stupid.

Once she forces my penis inside of her, there's no going back. It's already done. Her insides capture me, curl around me, suck me in deeper. There's no way I can stop this even if I tried.

She pants and moans, misting my neck with her kiwi-flavored saliva. But she doesn't fuck me like a human girl would fuck me. She doesn't ride on top of me or bounce up and down or bring me in and out. Instead, she clasps me in place, keeping me all the way inside and holding me there, her tail slithering against my thigh. But even without our bodies moving, there is still stimulation. It feels like her insides are filled with long gooey tendrils that tighten around my penis like a jellyfish capturing its prey. They rub against it, massaging it, coiling it up and jerking it off. It feels like I'm getting a hand job from a tiny mutant space squid that lives inside of her vagina, and it's better than any sensation I've ever felt in my life. Even when the tendrils insert themselves into my urethra and slither all the way down my urinary tract, it's still beyond heavenly.

Her body glows bright pink. If we weren't buried inside of this mushroom, she would have illuminated the entire forest. Perhaps that's why we had to be closed up in here, to prevent her light from drawing too much attention.

I lick her glowing skin, sucking her dusty, rubbery neck. She tastes earthy yet floral. She lays her head on me and her plant-like hair is itchy against my chest and tickles my neck and chin.

When I come, her body shivers and changes color, like she's climaxing with me. She moans like a crying alley cat and sprays her skunk musk all over me. I wrap my arms around her and squeeze her body against me, sucking sweet moisture from her neck.

After we finish, she doesn't release me, still holding me inside of her by sticky strings. She closes her eyes and curls her head into the crook of my neck. Our muscles relax. We hold each other, breathing against each other.

I inhale her fragrance and feel my mind drifting. Her smell is even more intoxicating after sex. It feels like I'm full of powerful painkillers, like I've just gone through surgery. My body doesn't feel capable of going anywhere. I just want to stay in this bed, wrapped around this weird alien woman for the rest of my life.

My penis is flaccid, but it's still inside of her, glued to her vaginal wall. I still feel movement curling around my shaft. It's not necessarily stimulating it, just moving around it gently. As my eyes drift shut and I begin to lose consciousness, I imagine my penis has been inserted into a pool of wiggling, squirming maggots. And for some reason I find that idea peaceful and comforting.

CHAPTER
FOUR

I wake up in a pool of warm mud, buried up to my neck. It takes me a few minutes before I realize I'm back in the hotel room. Mick's ass wiggles at me from the bathroom as he washes black muck from his body within the toilet waterfall.

I close my eyes and open them again, wondering how the hell I got here. The mud is actually a lot more soothing than I thought it would be. I feel weightless yet supported, wrapped up safely in a blanket of warm bubbling sludge. I don't want to get out. I just want to lie here all day.

When Mick sees that I'm awake, he says, "Time to get up. We've got work to do."

He enters the room, drying off with a towel he brought from home, not bothering to hide his junk as he talks to me.

"How'd I get here?" I ask, my voice feels weird and echoed.

He chuckles. "You don't remember?"

I shake my head.

"You were like a zombie," he says. "I found you wandering around naked in the parking lot. You were completely trashed."

"I remember having sex with this beautiful woman and then passing out."

"Beautiful woman?" He roars with laughter. "That wasn't a woman you were sleeping with. You definitely must have been trashed."

"What do you mean?"

"You were with a sex-slug," he says.

I shake my head. "No, not the slug. I didn't go near that slug. I left the room and found a different woman. She was hanging out on the back porch."

"There weren't any women there," he says. "They only had sex-slugs."

"No, there was this super hot nymph girl. She was amazing."

He shakes his head. "Nah, you must have imagined that. Sex-slugs are telepathic. They do whatever you want them to do, just by thinking about it. I bet it projected something into your mind so that you believed you were having sex with a woman, but were really just fucking a big sexy worm."

He licks his lips after he says the word *worm*.

I look down into the mud, wondering if it all could have been just a hallucination. But no, it's impossible. I clearly remember seeing the woman before I even encountered the slug. I clearly remember going outside and interacting with that woman.

"Man, was that an experience..." Mick says. "I

never thought I'd fuck anything like that…" He drops the towel and goes for his clothes. "I kind of wish I had a sex-slug of my very own."

After a shower and a weird fuzzy oatmeal-like breakfast, we take a slug-bus a couple hours out of town to meet with a tour guide who will be one of the guests on *Bizarre Foods*. His name is Bolgot and he's one of the only Kynarians Mick could find who's fluent in English.

"Bolgot, my man," Mick says, calling to a big yellow blob-like Kynarian the second we step off the slug-bus. "How's it going, bro?"

The creature turns around with a big round-toothed smile and oozes toward us, clomping on two stubby tree-trunk legs.

"Mr. Meyers," Bolgot says. His English pronunciation is perfect, but the strange gurgled tone of his Kynarian accent comes through. "Very nice to meet you again."

They tap heads when they meet, the traditional Kynarian greeting. Bolgot's large mushroom cap bounces off Mick's greasy skull. Then they shake hands.

Mick introduces me. "This is Rice. He'll be shooting for us this week."

Bolgot doesn't bounce his head against mine and opts to just shake my hand. "Very nice to meet you, Mr. Rice."

His pudgy marshmallow hand is too fat for me to wrap my fingers around and his fingers too stubby to wrap around mine, but I'm able to shake two of his digits well enough to call it a greeting.

All I say to him is "Hi." Then he turns back to Mick.

"Elder How is waiting for us on his property," Bolgot says. "We should go there as soon as we can."

"Elder How?" Mick asks. "He's the cluster fruit farmer, right?"

Bolgot nods. "He also has a few more delicacies I thought you might be interested in."

"Oh yeah, like what?" Mick asks.

"Well, for starters, he raises hogcocks," he says. "Have you heard of hogcocks?"

Mick shakes his head. "What are they?"

Bolgot smiles. "They'll be perfect for your show. You have nothing like them on Earth."

"Are they giant dicks with legs or something?" Mick asks.

He shakes his head. "No, they are amphibious pig-like mammals that have multiple eyeballs growing all over their body. Many different foods are made from them, but they are mostly bred for their eyeballs which are used in many stews and jellies. And because their eyes regenerate, it is a very stable food source in rural areas."

Mick nods, thinking it over. "Sounds promising. How come I've never heard of them before?"

"They're very rare, even to Kynarians," Bolgot says. "It's a bit like eating armadillo in the United States. Most Kynarians wouldn't even think to eat hogcock eyes, especially anyone from the city."

"Well, let's go check it out," Mick says.

Bolgot wraps his arm around Mick and leads him toward his snail-truck, leaving me to carry all of our equipment by myself.

The cluster fruit farm is amazing. Spiky blueberry-colored trees stretch for miles across the rolling landscape. Rainbow lollipop flowers speckle the fields of bubble grass. Kynarian workers walk on thirty-foot stilts, harvesting fruit with the precision of acrobats. It's one of the most breathtaking scenes I've seen since arriving on Kynaria.

"Rice, get some shots of this," Mick tells me, pointing at the fruit grove. "Get all of it."

"On it," I tell him.

I set two trunk-sized cases on the ground, pulling out the camera equipment. Four eye-shaped drones come to life the second I put the televisor over my eyes and flip on the control switch. I send them up into the air, hovering over the cluster fruit trees, recording as they go.

"Film everything you can," Mick says. "The workers. The fruit trees. The whole property. And definitely get the hogcocks if you can find them."

I just nod, too focused on directing four cameras at once to respond.

He says, "We're going to go meet with the old guy."

Then they leave me alone with my work.

Ever since the United Planets made first contact with Earth five years ago, there's been massive leaps in our technology. We went from cell phones and arguing with each other like idiots on the internet to teleporting across the galaxy and operating robots with our minds practically overnight. One day, all I had to worry about was holding a camera steady, and the next I had to learn how to become a one-man camera crew with a neuro-interface implanted into the side of my brain.

Using mostly just my thoughts, I'm able to pilot the four drones—or *eyebots* as Mick likes to call them—far over the cluster fruit farm, panning across the landscape and zooming in on the workers as they pick the spiky blue melon-sized fruits.

When I'm finished with the grove, I scan the air for any sign of the livestock. Since I've never seen a hogcock before, I have no idea what to be looking for other than some animal with a lot of eyes. I remember Bolgot saying they are amphibious, so I assume they'll be near some water.

I send one drone far behind the ranch, discovering a large gated area with a small pond and several fat pink frog-looking creatures wobbling along the water. Zooming in, they definitely have to be hogcocks. Their eyes are bigger than I expected, like grapefruit-sized fish eyes. They also are three times larger than the largest pigs back on Earth. I understand the resemblance, though. If I had to describe them to anyone I'd say they were frog-pigs covered in eyes.

As I pan across the hogcock pen, I see a woman walking among the beasts. She is pink and purple, exactly like the flowery woman I slept with last night. I zoom in on her. She's definitely the same species. She has the same skin, the same tail, the same blue leaf hair. She must be one of the farm workers.

I want Mick to see her. I want to show him that I really did sleep with a beautiful nymph woman last night and that she wasn't just some hallucinatory vision put in my head by a telepathic sex-slug.

I'm sure he'll be really impressed.

Down the hill, Mick and Bolgot are deep in conversation with some old mushroom man as they stroll through his property. I decide not to interrupt them and continue on my way, heading toward the back of the ranch to the hogcock pen.

But when I arrive, I don't see the flower woman anywhere. I just see the weird pig creatures blinking at me with their bunches of eyes. I send the eyebots to scan over me, but she seems to be gone. I wonder if maybe Mick was right. Maybe I did imagine her.

I look back and see Mick and the Kynarians heading toward me. Too bad the woman isn't here. They would have gotten here right in time. But before I give up, I catch a glimpse of her again from one of the eyebots.

She's rolling over a hogcock, trying to clean its belly or something.

A smile spreads across my face. I don't know why. These women are such perfect creatures. Being able to see one of them again brings me joy. Unfortunately, it also brings me another erection. I try to cover it up before the other men arrive.

Her scent fills the air and I breathe it in deeply. This woman smells different from the one last night. Her scent is richer, more robust. It kind of reminds me of lilac and cardamom.

I go to the fence and climb up to get a better look at her, but when I see her I'm so shocked I nearly drop the eyebots out of the air.

"What the fuck…" I say.

The woman is on top of one of the hogcocks, straddling it, rubbing against it. My first thought is that she's trying to hold it down, maybe to pull out an infected tooth or trim its nails. But then I realize her skin is illuminated as she presses herself against the animal's greasy belly. She's fucking it. Just as the woman had done with me last night, she is making love to this horrific eyeball-pig creature.

When Mick and the Kynarians get to me, Mick yells, "What the hell are you doing up there, Rice?"

I don't know what to say. My mouth is just hanging open.

I point my finger at the mushroom nymph and say, "She… She is…" But that's all I can get out.

When the old farmer sees what I'm pointing at, he

freaks out. Even though I can't understand Kynarian I can tell that he's absolutely pissed. If that woman actually is one of his field hands and is having sex with his livestock, I imagine he'd be pretty pissed off about it.

Elder How grabs what looks to be a fire extinguisher from the side of the fence and races into the pen. He sprays the woman until she rolls off of the hogcock and runs away. He chases after her, spraying her until she's soaked.

"What's going on?" Mick asks, trying to climb up on the fence with me to get a better look.

Through the drone cameras, I'm able to see that the old farmer isn't actually spraying the nymph with water. It's some kind of corrosive poison. As she tries to run away, her leaf-like hair falls out, her skin melts from her body, her muscles slide off her bones.

I don't know what to do except stand here as the farmer murders the beautiful woman right in front of us. Her high-pitched screams fill the air. It's like I'm watching a pre-abolition slave getting executed by a plantation owner for stealing a loaf of bread. When the woman falls on the ground, he continues spraying her until she doesn't move anymore, until she's just a puddle of soup in the dirt.

As Elder How leaves the pen, he takes the hogcock that the woman slept with and separates it from the others.

"What the hell was that?" Mick asks.

Bolgot translates and the old Kynarian responds.

"He says it was a jelly bug," Bolgot tells us. "They're horrible, disgusting creatures."

"What the hell's a jelly bug?" Mick asks.

"It's an invasive species that showed up within the past few years," Bolgot says. "They were accidentally introduced to our eco-system by travelers from some other world. Now they're wreaking havoc across the countryside."

"What do they do?" Mick asks.

"They breed with the livestock and spread all sorts of horrible diseases. They're very dangerous. Elder How has lost thirty of his herd to jelly bugs in this season alone."

As I hear this, my hands shiver. My skin crawls. I nearly crash an eyebot into a tree. I'm not sure I heard this correctly. Are they saying that the woman I slept with last night was one of these jelly bugs?

"Wait…" I say to Bolgot. "I saw it. That was no bug. It was a woman. It looked almost human."

Bolgot shakes his head. "Don't let its looks fool you. It's not an intelligent species. It's not a woman. Jelly bugs are vermin. They're like rats and they're very, very dangerous. If you ever see one you should exterminate it right away."

"But…" I begin, wanting to tell them all about my encounter last night and how I slept with one of them, thinking she was a normal woman.

Mick cuts me off, "So are there more of them out there? Are we safe?"

Bolgot nods. "They only go after pets, livestock, and wild animals. They've never attacked a Kynarian before."

"What about a human?" Mick asks.

Bolgot shakes his head. "I doubt they'd have any interest in humans either. They prefer dumb, small mammals that won't fight back."

Before I'm able to tell them about my experience, they change the subject and saunter away. I'm too embarrassed to explain what happened now. But after what they said, my mind is racing. What exactly are jelly bugs? Where did they come from? How come they look human, like intelligent beings? Why are they dangerous? Is it just because they are diseased or because of other reasons? Am I lucky to have survived last night?

I look over at Elder How. He raises a long bladed tool that resembles a scythe. Then he lowers it into the squirming animal by his feet, chopping off its head. When Bolgot sees me staring at the old farmer, it's like he can tell that I want to ask why the hogcock had to be killed.

Bolgot answers the question before I have to ask. "Once the jelly bug gets to it, it can't be saved. The meat is spoiled now."

I nod at him and calmly walk away, trying not to expose the whirlwind of panic that spins through my head.

For the rest of the shoot, I can't focus. The eyebots fly around on their own without me putting much attention into the shots they capture. Doing a good job doesn't concern me at the moment. I keep thinking about the creature I slept with last night. I thought I was with a beautiful woman, but it was really like I fucked a rat or a cockroach. And because I didn't wear a condom, who knows what weird diseases I caught from it.

I do feel nauseous. It's more likely that I feel this way due to being hungover than because of some alien disease I might have caught last night, but it does make me feel at least a little bit paranoid. A part of me feels that the nausea comes not from the alcohol I drank, but from the jelly bug's intoxicating fragrance. It's like my body is going through withdrawal.

But I really should go to a doctor and get checked out. I could have something serious. It might even be curable if caught in time. The only problem is where I go. Do I try to find a Kynarian doctor or go back to Earth? Kynarian doctors won't know much or anything about human physiology, yet Earth doctors won't know much or anything about the diseases jelly bugs carry. Either way, I need to make my decision soon.

CHAPTER
FIVE

It's nightfall and my nausea has become unbearable. What started as a slight queasiness reminiscent of a mild hangover has turned into what I imagine heroin withdrawal must feel like—worse than any flu or any food poisoning, and all I want to do is get some more of the drug that made me this way.

All day, we went from shoot to shoot, location to location, and I did my best to do my job while suffering through dizzying pain and throwing up every ten minutes. I was hardly able to keep myself standing for most of it.

Now I'm sitting with Bolgot and Mick at a restaurant downtown, wondering how I'm going to keep down any food. The place is supposed to be special, one of the main restaurants Mick wants to use on the show. I'm sweating and shaking in my seat. I've been breathing in so many spores throughout the day that my sinuses are clogged. Watery snot runs down my nostrils but I'm in too much discomfort to wipe it away. The two people at the table don't seem to notice anything is wrong with me.

A toadstool waitress comes to us and brings us menus.

She is a curvy woman with smooth yellow skin and a brown-speckled bell-shaped head. Unlike other Kynarians, she looks more human proportionately. She wears a tight pink outfit that exposes her bulging fungal breasts. Mick checks her out as she hovers over the table, unable to conceal his slobbering expressions.

"Man…" he says, admiring her cleavage.

Mick Meyers is one of the most shameless, most sleazy douchebags I've ever met. I kind of hate him. But despite my criticisms of the guy, it's me who has an erection while sitting in her presence.

"Hey," I say as I pick up a menu. "I thought Kynarian restaurants don't let you order your own food?"

Milk runs out of my nose.

"Ahh, not usually," Mick says. "But this restaurant is special."

The waitress pulls out a thin needle-shaped knife and stabs me in the arm with it.

"Ow!" I cry.

I look at the others, rubbing my bicep. The waitress sticks another knife inside of Mick.

"What the hell was that for?" I ask.

Mick just laughs at me, but won't explain.

He just says, "You'll see."

We let Bolgot order our food for us. The menu has no pictures and I have no idea how to read Kynarian. The language doesn't even have letters or characters of any kind. It's just one long squiggly line going up and down the page.

When the food comes, it looks a lot like a sandwich but with some kind of mushroom instead of bread. The meat is sizzling. It looks more like Earth food than the dinner I had yesterday.

"I ordered you something I thought you might be comfortable with," Bolgot says to me. "I lived on Earth for three years, so I know what Earthers like."

I nod my head and look down at the plate. I have no idea how I'm going to eat it. I'm so sick to my stomach that just the appearance of it makes me want to throw up.

"Take a bite," Mick says, smiling with anticipation.

His excitement worries me.

"Why?" I say. "What is it?"

He giggles. "Just do it!"

Even though I'm nauseous, there's no way I'm going to get away with not eating it. I at least have to take a bite.

I sink my teeth into the mushroom-meat sandwich and chew. It tastes kind of gamey but it's not that bad. It doesn't taste anything like beef. More like greasy wild boar. If I wasn't sick I might even like it.

"How do you like it?" Mick asks, still smirking.

"It's fine," I say.

"Do you know what it is?" he asks.

I shrug.

"It's you!" he cries.

He slams his hand on the table and laughs his head off. I have no idea what he's talking about.

"It's me?" I ask.

"It's your own meat," he says. "You're eating yourself."

I'm still confused. Bolgot has to step in to explain it.

"This restaurant clones your flesh and turns it into fine cuisine," Bolgot says. "When the waitress poked you in the arm, it was to get a sample of your DNA. They rapid-grow the meat in the back and cook it up for you."

I look down at the sandwich, examining the gray meat. I can't believe it's me. This is what it would taste like if somebody murdered me and turned my flesh into dinner. Not only that, but it's human flesh. This is what human flesh tastes like. The greasy, porky flavor lingers on my tongue and I have to do everything possible to keep from throwing up right on the floor.

Mick takes three massive bites of his sandwich and chews with his mouth open, moaning in pleasure at the taste.

"Oh man..." he says, talking with his mouth full. "This is good Mick Burger."

When I put my sandwich down and push the plate away, Mick laughs and keeps on eating.

Bolgot doesn't have a plate of food. He just sits at the table, watching us eat. Because Mick is busy slobbering over his self-food, I engage the Kynarian in conversation.

"You didn't want to get anything?" I ask.

Bolgot shakes his head. "No, it's very expensive. Kynarians usually only eat at cloning restaurants for special occasions."

"Like anniversaries?" I ask.

"Quite the opposite, actually," he says. "First dates."

"First dates?"

He nods. "When two Kynarians have a physical attraction to each other, it is customary for them to go on a first date at a cloning restaurant. Only you don't eat a meal made from your own flesh. You eat the cloned flesh of your date."

My jaw goes slack. The idea of eating my own meat disturbs the hell out of me, but thinking about how awkward it would be to eat the meat of a person sitting across from me is even worse. Not to mention watching them eat your flesh in front of you.

"The purpose is to see if you're compatible with each other," Bolgot says. "Many Kynarians believe that if your date's flesh tastes good to you and you taste good to them, then you are well-matched and should continue dating. If you don't like each other's taste then the relationship is ended there."

I look around the restaurant and notice that most of the people eating here are couples on first dates. Most of them seem to be having a good time together. I don't see anyone disgusted by their food, though I don't see anyone absolutely delighted in their meals either.

I ask, "But what if you get a really terrible chef that day and he ruins your meal?"

Bolgot nods. "Yes, that's why only the best chefs work in cloning restaurants. It is also common for males to give large tips to their chef before the meal is prepared so that he puts extra care into doing a good job."

When the waitress comes back, Mick flirts with her. Even though she doesn't speak English, he's able to hit on her with horrible pick-up lines using only his translation device. I try to block him out and just focus on the Kynarian man.

"But sometimes a chef ruins a meal and it results in ending a relationship before it even begins," Bolgot continues. "If a couple believes their chef was at fault and they believe they would have enjoyed eating their date's flesh if it were prepared properly, couples sometimes will go to a different restaurant and try again. If they enjoy their flesh the second time it will usually disgrace their original chef. In extreme cases, he will very likely be embarrassed into retirement."

I nod. I couldn't imagine having to go through that every time you went on a first date with somebody.

"It's just a tradition, though," Bolgot says. "A lot of people don't really believe it. I have plenty of friends who are happily married despite being disturbed by their spouse's taste."

I look up at Mick who is still giggling and flirting with the Kynarian waitress. He holds up the burger of himself, trying to get her to taste it.

"Come on, try it," he says, gripping her by the elbow. "I'm delicious."

She shakes her head, trying to get back to work. But Mick doesn't take no for an answer.

"Just try it," he says, his translation device spewing back his voice in Kynarian. "If you don't like me I'll leave you alone."

The woman gives in and takes a small bite, just so that she can get rid of him. He lets go of her and she turns and races away. But she only gets ten feet. When she turns back, I watch her savoring the flavor in her mouth with a big round-toothed smile on her mushroom face. She races back to Mick and wants to take another, much larger, bite. I'm not sure if it's because she likes Mick or because human meat is delicious to Kynarians.

As she's gobbling on his flesh, Mick looks at us and says, "See? I'm delicious. Everyone should eat my meat."

He slams his hand on the table and chuckles.

Then he says, "I'm going to bring this technology back to Earth and open up my own chain of restaurants that *only* sells food made with my meat." He laughs again. "It'll be great. And there'll be pictures of me all over the menu so that everyone knows whose meat they're eating."

Bolgot and I just nod at him. We have no idea if he's joking or serious.

Snot keeps flowing out of my nose. The pressure inside my head is killing me. My brain feels itchy, like it's on fire.

"You're bleeding," Bolgot says, pointing at my face.

When I rub my nostril, I notice that my stream of snot has turned into blood.

"Sorry…" I say, embarrassed to be bleeding at the table.

I hold my nose tightly with a furry napkin for a few minutes, but it doesn't stop.

"Are you okay?" Bolgot asks. His voice stresses genuine concern. "I know what it's like trying to adjust to the climate on another planet. My first few months on Earth were not pretty at all."

"I'm sure I'll be fine," I say.

Although Bolgot is concerned by my unending nosebleed, Mick doesn't even notice. He's still messing with the waitress. Only now she's not annoyed by his advances. She's sitting down at the table with us, flirting back. Her rubbery knees rubbing against his thigh.

I wait a few more minutes, but the blood won't stop. I get out of my seat.

"I'm going to go to the bathroom," I tell Bolgot.

He nods with understanding.

The bathroom is filled with a row of waterfalls. A large orange Kynarian male is bathing in one on the end, brown ooze leaking from his skin as he washes. It is a unisex bathroom as all bathrooms are on Kynaria, but there aren't any women in here at the moment.

I go to one of the waterfalls and rinse the blood off of my nose. The Kynarian looks at me like I'm a crazy person for using it without taking off my clothes or stepping all the way inside.

When I stick my finger in my nostril, I feel lumps inside. It's like I've got marble-sized boogers trapped in there. I blow my nose hard and dig one of the bloody globs out, but it's not a booger. It's something else.

I squeeze the slimy chunk while washing it off. It

feels like a spongy piece of meat, like a part of my nasal cavity wall had broken off inside of my nose. But once I rinse the blood away, I see that it is bulb-shaped with pink and white speckles. It's a tiny mushroom.

I put my finger in my nose again and feel around. There are more of them. Mushrooms are growing inside of me. I go to the mirror and take a closer look. Dozens of tiny toadstools are clustered inside, covered in mucus. A thick milk gushes out as I press too firmly on the nostrils.

"What the fuck…" I say, wondering how the hell they got there. "Mushrooms?"

I've got a fucking mushroom infection. I don't know if it was caused from the spores I've been breathing in, like it's the Kynarian equivalent to seasonal allergies, or if it's something I got from my encounter with the jelly bug. It could be some kind of alien disease she gave me.

The fungus isn't only growing inside my nostrils. I can feel them throughout my entire nasal passageway, spreading into my sinus cavities and all the way to the back of my ear canals. I can feel a collection of them in the hollow space behind my left eyeball, scratching against the optic nerve whenever the eye rolls inside its socket. They're even in my throat, heading toward my lungs.

The speed at which they've spread is mindboggling, but I remember toadstools growing on my lawn practically overnight back on Earth. If the mushrooms sprout this quickly, what's going to happen in a couple more days? What's going to happen in a week? The mushrooms could grow so large that they block my airways, fill my lungs and suffocate me. Or maybe they'll just grow right into my brain and kill me that way. Either way, I need to get to a hospital immediately.

Before I leave the bathroom, I decide I should take a piss first. I've had to go ever since I've gotten there, but have been worried about using public Kynarian bathrooms since I heard about them.

I probably shouldn't just stand outside of the shower and piss into it. I'm pretty sure that's not acceptable behavior. But with the big Kynarian man watching me, I don't really want to get naked and shower next to him. I consider waiting until he's done, but he could be going for a long time. He seems to be excreting a lot of sludge from his body. I wonder if the taste of his date didn't agree with him.

After debating it for another minute, I decide I can't hold it any longer. I remove my clothes and put them on hooks near the mirror. Then I crawl inside the basin on the other end, away from the Kynarian.

But once I'm in the water, letting the warmth wash over me, I can't get myself to piss. I wonder if it's the Kynarian watching me. I wonder if he's giving me the bashful bladder. But then my penis starts to hurt. It feels like pressure is building up, as if I actually am pissing but there's something inside my urethra, blocking the urine stream.

I squeeze the shaft of my penis and feel lumps inside.

There are five lumps, most of them collected near the base.

"Shit…" I say.

The pain builds as my urine stream continues to be blocked. It burns all the way to my bladder. I squeeze on the lumps and they move. Something is inside it. The mushrooms must also be growing through my urinary tract. I squeeze again, pushing the mushroom bulbs upward.

I cry out at the burning pain, still trying to urinate, wondering if I can piss them out like kidney stones. But the panic hits me even harder than the pain. If there are mushrooms growing in my nose and inside of my penis, that must mean they are spreading throughout my entire body. They're probably growing through my stomach and intestines. They're probably growing around my heart, spreading through the blood.

Squeezing my shaft like a tube of toothpaste, milk oozes out of the tip of my dick, spilling onto the floor of the water basin. I continue applying pressure, trying to force the mushrooms out. The first one comes out as mush, just a brown paste that doesn't resemble anything anymore. But it does have a very strong fungal aroma, like a yeast infection on a dead pig. I immediately rinse my hands off in the flowing water after I smell it.

Next to me, the Kynarian watches me, wondering what I'm doing. He probably knows nothing about how humans go to the bathroom, so this could be how we shit for all he knows. But something in his eyes makes me think that I'm doing something offensive. So offensive that he wants to throw me out of the bathroom or stomp me into the floor. But I'm in too much pain to worry about that.

The next lump resists, like it's still attached to the inside of my urethral walls. I grip the flesh beneath the lump and push upward until I feel a tearing sensation and blood oozes out with the milk. But I ignore the blood, push past the pain and keep tugging. Once the lump reaches the opening, I notice it's not the same as the last one. It's not just brown fungal mush. It's gray and crusty, like a large chunk of scab.

But once I force it out, the thing crawls across the tip of my penis. I scream and brush it away. The creature scurries across the basin floor.

"What the fuck!" I cry.

My voice echoes through the bathroom. I nearly slip and fall out of the tub onto the hard floor. The Kynarian male is so angry with my outburst that he grunts, screams something in his language—obviously a profanity—and then he gets out of the water, unable to continue using the bathroom in peace.

I look down at the bug that came out of me. It scuttles through the pooling water on the basin floor. The thing is a small crustacean, like a roly poly or a baby shrimp.

"Are you kidding me…"

That was inside of my penis. How the fuck did it get in there? Was it the nymph woman? Was her vagina filled with bugs when I fucked her? Was she full of tiny shrimp-like parasites?

When I feel the shaft of my penis, I realize that it wasn't the only one. The three remaining lumps feel exactly the same as the last one did. They have the same crusty, tearing sensation when I touch them. They twist and curl within me, burrowing down the urethra into my bladder. I'm sure there's even more than three deeper inside of me.

I need to get them out.

After what feels like a gallon of blood and milk and brown fungus paste, I eventually squeeze all of the crustaceans out of me. At least all of the ones I can reach. Weak and shivering, I dry off and dress and return to the table with Bolgot and Mick, only Mick isn't there anymore.

I sit down.

"Where's Meyers?" I ask, still out of breath from my experience in the bathroom.

"The waitress was done with her shift, so he left with her," Bolgot says.

I nod. I'm perfectly fine with that. I need to get to a hospital and would rather go with Bolgot anyway. He seems like he'd be of better help.

"Are you okay?" Bolgot asks. "You were in the bathroom for a very long time."

I shake my head and lower my eyes.

"About that…" I begin.

But with my eyes on the table, I notice that somebody has taken a large bite out of my sandwich. Because I wasn't going to eat it, I shouldn't mind. But it was made of my flesh. Somebody eating a sandwich made of my flesh without my permission seems like it should be impolite. I kind of feel violated. I'm guessing it was Mick who wanted the taste, maybe to compare it to his own meat.

"Yes?" Bolgot asks.

I shake the distraction out of my thoughts.

"I think I need to go to a hospital," I tell him.

His bulgy eyes get bulgier. "What's wrong?"

I shake my head, not knowing where to start. I'm not sure I feel comfortable mentioning the bugs or even the mushroom infection. I decide I better just go straight for my main concern.

"I slept with a jelly bug," I say.

When I say the word, he shushes me, telling me to keep my voice down. Like jelly bug is a dirty word or something.

He wants me to clarify. "Did you say jelly bug?"

I nod. "That creature Elder How killed back on the cluster fruit farm. You called it a jelly bug. Well, last night I had sex with one. I thought she was a woman."

His face is filled with dread.

"You have to be joking…" he says.

"No, I'm serious."

"How could you have sex with one of those things? That's disgusting."

"I thought she was beautiful."

When he hears me use the word *beautiful* to describe it, he cringes like I just said something horribly offensive, like I just called a dung beetle *sexy*.

"But they are vermin… They are like Earth cockroaches."

79

"She looked more human than Kynarians do."

"It doesn't matter what she looks like," he says. "Would you mate with a rodent if it looked like a human female?"

I shrug. "I guess not. But at the time I didn't know."

He waves the conversation away, realizing it's not important why I did it. It's already done and there's no going back.

"How do you feel?" he asks. "Are you sick?"

I nod my head, but don't get into the details.

He sighs at me and then drops into deep thought.

"So what do I do?" I ask.

He shakes his head. "I'm not sure. Jelly bugs usually only go after animals. It's never happened with intelligent beings before. Normally, we just put down infected livestock. We don't try to save them."

"So there's nothing I can do?"

He takes another long pause to think.

"You have to go back to Earth," he says. "Leave Kynaria immediately."

I'm surprised by his words. "Leave the planet?"

"Right now. Get a ticket to Earth and go to a human hospital."

"Why can't I go to a Kynarian hospital?"

He shakes his head. "They'll just put you in quarantine. They'll think you're a pervert or think humans are a primitive subspecies that isn't worth saving. They'll show you no sympathy." He gets to his feet and stands me up. "Human doctors will at least do everything they can to save you."

My hands are trembling as he tells me this. He tries

to hold me steady.

He says, "Don't worry about the show. Just get out of here. The longer you're in Kynaria the more danger you'll be in."

I don't say another word. He walks me out the door and puts me on a slug-taxi. I don't even think about doing anything else but follow his advice.

Back in the hotel room, Mick has company over. The waitress from the cloning restaurant is with him, her clothes spread across the floor. I don't bother being polite and race through the room toward my luggage. Mick and the woman are naked in the pool of mud, moaning, writhing together. The Kynarian's naked flesh is pale and puffy. It makes it appear as though Mick is fucking a giant marshmallow.

"Where the hell are you going?" Mick asks me.

He doesn't seem bothered to start up a conversation while in the middle of having sex. The Kynarian woman also doesn't seem to mind, continuing to bounce and wiggle against him as though sexual intercourse around other people isn't uncommon in their culture.

"I'm leaving," I say.

Mick looks over the woman's shoulder and glares at me. "What did you say?"

I pack clothes from the bathroom into my luggage as I say, "I'm going back to Earth."

"No…" Mick says, finally pushing the woman off of him. "You're staying here. You've got a job to do."

I shake my head. "I've got to get to the hospital."

Mick swims through the mud toward me. The woman stays wrapped around him, riding on his back, squeezing his leathery flesh against hers.

"What's wrong with you?" he asks.

I don't bother explaining it to him. I don't have time. After I finish packing, I realize I've forgotten something.

"Shit…" I say.

I pat down my pockets and then dig through my coat. Then I reopen my luggage and tear furiously through my clothes.

"My passport…" I say. "Where the fuck is my passport?"

Mick rolls over in the muck and nibbles on the mushroom girl's neck. "How should I know?"

"Did you do anything with it?" he asks.

He shrugs. "No."

"I had it yesterday…" I say.

But the outfit I was wearing yesterday isn't here anymore.

"What happened to the clothes from last night?" I ask Mick.

He doesn't seem to care enough to answer, completely over the fact that I'm abandoning the show and focused more on the woman again.

"You said you found me naked outside the brothel," I tell him. "What did you do with the clothes I was wearing?"

Mick just snorts a laugh. "I never found your clothes.

I brought you back naked."

"Are you serious?" I cry.

He doesn't answer, dunking his head in the mud to lick the girl's sludgy breasts.

When I realize I have to go all the way back to the sex-slug brothel to find it, I say, "Fuck…"

I don't have a choice. I have to go back there. They'll never let me teleport back to Earth without it.

On the way out the door, I call out, "Tell Andrew Zimmern I'm sorry."

But Mick is too deep in the mud to hear me.

CHAPTER
SIX

I take a slug-taxi toward the brothel outside of town. The place is an hour away. I wanted to get off this planet as soon as possible, but now I probably won't leave until late tonight. I don't even know if there will be any more trips to Earth available by the time I get to the transport station. I could be stuck here until tomorrow. And if trips between Kynaria and Earth aren't very popular, I could be stuck here for days. I might even have to go to a completely new planet for treatment if there's no way I can get to Earth soon enough.

But I'm not too worried about transportation right now. I'll figure that out later. Right now, I'm more worried about running into the nymph girl again. Now that I know what she is, the idea of encountering her out in the mushroom forest terrifies me. I'm more than likely going to run into her. I'm sure my clothes are still in the same place where I took them off. They're going to be on the floor of her mushroom burrow, probably covered in tiny crustaceans and saturated in her musk. But there's a chance that they won't be there. There's a chance that in my drunken stupor I took them with me and lost them somewhere in the woods. If they're not in her burrow I might never find them.

While thinking of seeing the woman again, my penis becomes erect. Only it is the most painful erection I've ever had in my life. I feel hard crusty nuggets crawling up my urethra. It feels like my urinary tract has become one long scab that breaks apart as my penis hardens. I try ignoring my memory of the woman, try to think of something mundane to cause the swelling to go down. But the deeper the slug-taxi drives into the wilderness, the more I'm reminded of her.

I swear I can smell her aroma in the forest outside. I'm not sure if it's hers or other jelly bugs trying to lure in potential mates, but the scent makes it impossible to get rid of the erection. I can't ease the pain. But I've got to push forward. Once I get through this I can go back home and never leave the planet again.

When the slug-taxi arrives in front of the brothel, I try sending it telepathic messages. I want to tell the slug to wait for me. I want it to know that I'll be right back. But the taxi is unable to communicate a denial or confirmation. I just have to hope it knows to stay for me. Last night, I went home unconscious. I have no idea how Mick got us back to our hotel room. If he had the bartender call us a slug-taxi then I have no idea how I'll get home. I don't have a translation device like Mick so I won't be able to communicate with him.

I guess it doesn't matter anyway. By the looks of the brothel, it appears to be closed. There are no slug-cars in the parking lot. There are no lights through the windows. I am all alone out here.

Stepping down from the slug-taxi, I look back at it and say, "Stay. I'll just be ten minutes. Don't go anywhere."

The slug just looks at me with long gooey eyes.

I step slowly away from the slug, waiting to lunge for it if it tries to leave. I'd rather go back to the city without my passport than get stuck out here overnight. The taxi doesn't go anywhere. I take a few more steps back. It doesn't leave. I think it's going to wait for me.

As I walk around the side of the building, I look back every twenty feet, just to make sure the slug doesn't go anywhere. It seems to have understood my request. I just hope it'll stay long enough for me to find my passport.

Finding the burrow isn't as easy as I thought it would be. I was drunk last night and wasn't really paying attention to where I was going. I don't even remember the area where I first encountered the creature. The mushroom trees all look the same. There aren't any distinguishing landmarks.

Stepping into a dark alien forest is a lot more terrifying now than it was last night. Last time, I was with a woman, or something I thought was a woman. I felt safe with her, like she knew what she was doing. Mick said the planet has giant man-eating spiders. Without the girl to guide me, there's a good chance I might step into a massive web or become some wild creature's lunch.

I wander in the dark for several minutes and realize I'd better hurry if I'm going to get back before the slug-taxi leaves me. The only thing I can think to do is try to find the girl again, try to get her to lead me back to her bed.

"Hello?" I call out. "Are you out there?"

I know she won't understand me, but there's a possibility that she'll remember my voice and show herself. But I don't see anything out here. I only hear the wind blowing through the mushroom caps, the fluttering of large bird-sized moths, and hundreds of croaking frog-like creatures somewhere in the distance.

Then a thought hits me. Bolgot said that you should immediately kill any jelly bug you come across. If this is true, it's possible that the brothel's bartender could have exterminated them by now. They were hanging around his establishment. He might have killed them soon after we left last night. His business might even be closed today just to handle the extermination. But, then again, the brothel didn't seem like the kind of place that was well-kept. The mud was old. The building was filthy. He probably didn't bother dealing with any of the vermin he had hanging around.

I wonder if I shouldn't go back to the brothel and see if the women weren't hanging out on the back porch, or maybe see if their corpses weren't somewhere closer to the property. There might even be jelly bug traps laid out nearby. But just before I make up my mind, a wind picks up and blows against my face. And on the wind is the flowery scent of the woman from last night.

She's here, somewhere. I don't see her but she has to be near. I'm not sure if it is her or another jelly bug, but there's a part of me that is certain that it's the same woman. The aroma is exactly the same as what I smelled last night. Because the other jelly bug I encountered earlier today had a different smell, I'm sure they each have their own unique scent.

"Hello?" I call out. "Are you out here?"

I head into the wind, trying to follow the odor. Her scent becomes stronger.

"Hello?"

The sound of twigs breaking causes me to take pause. The leaves of overgrown bushes rustle like something is coming through them toward me.

"Is that you?" I ask.

I move closer to the bushes, smelling the air. My erection digs into my pants as I bend down to get a better look. Her scent becomes stronger but I'm not sure it's her. It could be anything. I don't want to get too close and have some strange alien beast lunge out at me. The bushes rustle again.

Upon closer examination, the bush is the same blue-leafed plant that grows from the woman's head like hair. It's very possible that she would be hiding here, since it is the perfect camouflage. But I don't see anything inside. I don't hear anymore rustling.

"Hello?" I call out.

While looking at the blue bushes, I wonder why the nymph has hair that matches its leaves. Her species comes from a different world. She wouldn't have evolved with these plants. I wonder if it is just a coincidence and maybe there are plants like this on her home world as well. Or perhaps they evolve quickly and have already adapted to the Kynarian environment in just a few short years. If so I wonder how long their lifecycle is. If they breed like rats or cockroaches they might reach maturity within weeks or days. Three years might have been many generations ago for this species. They might have adapted to this environment very quickly.

"Where are you?" I say to the bushes.

I give up and stand up straight. Then I nearly shriek as I see movement in the corner of my eye. When I turn, she's there, staring at me with her red eyes. She was creeping up on me. The second I turn to her she freezes in her tracks.

It's just how it was last night. Only now that I know what she is, her movements make more sense. She moves like an animal. She creeps up on me like a raccoon searching for food scraps in a driveway.

"There you are," I say.

She's not as afraid of me as she was yesterday. She doesn't run away and hide. But she's still cautious. She doesn't approach me too quickly. Her eyes locked on mine, examining my every move.

"Come on," I say. "Lead me to your home."

But instead of leading me away, she comes toward

me. I take a step back. I don't want to get too close to her.

"Don't touch me," I say. "I'll follow you."

But she doesn't understand. She slinks closer, taking small quiet steps. When she moves a little nearer, I hear the glands in her armpits spray. Her aroma carries on the wind and hits me with such force it makes my eyes water.

I draw a deep breath and close my eyes, taking in the intoxicating fumes. Then I shake my head. I snap out of it. I try rubbing the smell from my nose. She steps closer and sprays again. I plug my nose but it doesn't help. As the scent invades my senses, I no longer feel any pain. I can't feel the creatures crawling inside of my urethra. I can't feel the mushrooms growing within my respiratory system. And my sickness has been entirely washed away. My nausea was definitely caused by withdrawal from her aromatic drug. Now that I've ingested it again, I feel much, much better. I feel euphoric. The next thing I know, I'm releasing my nose and taking in another deep breath of her perfume.

She approaches me again. This time I don't step away. I let her come for me. She rubs my erection through my pants, scratching at it like a cat on a door. When I unzip my pants, she pulls out my dick and strokes it. I look down and see several lumps on my shaft where tiny crustaceans burrow beneath my skin. She weaves her fingers between the lumps, caressing them. It's almost like she's trying to soothe the creatures inside.

"What the hell am I doing…" I say, trying to snap myself out of it.

I just need her to lead me back to her burrow so I

can get my passport. Then I have to leave. I can't let this creature touch me anymore. She's diseased. She's vermin.

But when I look at her hands rubbing against me, I wonder how she can possibly be vermin. Her fingers are so human, so smooth. She is nothing like a rat or a cockroach. She's just like me. I wonder if the Kynarians are mistaken. Maybe she really is an intelligent species. Maybe they just don't understand her kind. Just because they live in the forest and aren't civilized doesn't mean they're animals.

Then I look up at her face and see tiny crustaceans crawl across her cheek and through her leaf-like hair. She doesn't even bat an eye when one of them crawls up her nose. It's like she has an entire colony of them living inside her.

Now that I'm properly saturated in her drug, she leads me back to her burrow. I follow her like a zombie through the mushrooms, staggering in a drunken haze. I try to focus on my passport. I just need to get the passport. If I linger too long, my ride is going to take off without me.

"You're weird…" I say to the girl as I crawl inside of her home. I'm not sure why I say it. I'm feeling really drunk.

Once inside, the place is larger than I remember. The ground is more solid. But it's too dark to see. I feel around the floor for my old clothes, but I can't find them.

If I just find my pants I can run away.

The nymph starts filling in the hole. Like a groundhog, she kicks the dirt with her hind legs, shoving mud and forest debris into the opening to enclose us within. I try to stop her. I push on the wall, trying to break it down. I don't want to be trapped in here with her. She tries to push me back and prevent me from breaking it down, but I won't stop. I shove her slender arms out of my way and kick the wall down. I don't care if I hurt her or scare her. Now that I'm back inside her burrow, I don't need her anymore. I hope she runs away.

Then I hear a squirting sound and moisture hits me directly in the face. It's so dark that I didn't see it coming. She must have put her stink gland right in my face. My brain rolls and my eyes spin. It's like somebody hit me in the head with a grenade filled with morphine. While I'm dazed, the jelly bug fills in the hole, closing us tightly inside the room together.

I can't see anything. I move my fingers around the floor, fumbling through a fuzzy insect-filled nest, trying to find my passport. But my clothes don't seem to be here. I need to be able to see.

"Got a light?" I ask her, slurring my words and giggling to myself.

But then I remember. She does have a light. Her skin lights up when I touch her.

I feel my way to her and grab hold of her arm. Then I rub it up the shoulder, but nothing happens. I rub her knee and push on her chest. I shove my palm into her face. But nothing happens. She doesn't seem to light up at all.

"Why won't you turn on?"

Perhaps it's the way I touch her. Remembering last night, she didn't light up from just being touched. She lit up from sexual stimulation. I have to put her in the mood to lighten the room.

But I don't want to go down that road. I already have an erection poking into my stomach. I already am drunk on lust. If I get into it any more than this I won't be able to turn back.

The woman makes the decision for me. She comes to me, grabbing at my penis. I lick her neck and caress her shoulders. She lights up slightly, but not enough to see anything. I stroke my hand up her breasts and rub oil out of her nipple. It still doesn't do much.

Sitting up close to her in the dark, I can feel her warmth radiating against me. I wonder why she's called a jelly bug. She's no bug. She's warm-blooded. She's beautiful. While in the dark, she might as well be a human woman.

As I caress her skin, I lean in to her neck and inhale her scent. Her skin glows brighter. Her face lights up. She stares at me with her deep red eyes. I lean in and smell her again, this time slower. I savor every particle of it. Her skin grows even brighter.

That's what it is. She's aroused when I smell her. It's

more sensual to her than being touched, more titillating than when I kiss her neck. Maybe it's a turn on to watch someone enjoy your scent. Maybe it makes her feel desired and beautiful. Whatever the case, I now know how to brighten the room.

I keep smelling her as I scan the ground around me. There's no sign of my clothes. I keep looking. I keep sniffing. But there's nothing. My clothes aren't here.

Then I realize something: I'm not in the right burrow.

I look around to be sure, but it's true. This isn't the same hole I was in last night. It's completely different. Breaking away from the woman, I feel the floor, digging under the fuzzy bed just to be sure. But there's no denying it. She took me to a different mushroom.

But why would she take me to a different burrow? I stare at her, examining her face. I wonder if she's not even the same woman I was with last night. She might be a completely different girl. But she looks exactly like the other one. They have the same red eyes. They have the same body proportions, the same smell. She also wasn't as afraid of me tonight, like she was familiar with me. She wouldn't have been so brave if we were meeting for the first time. But if it is her, then why a different burrow? Do they dig multiple burrows all over the forest? It might make it easier for them to capture mates if they had more than just one to bring them to.

PARASITE MILK

Either way, I need to get out of here. I need to find the burrow from last night. It might be near this one. I might still be able to find it.

I push the nymph away as she struggles with my pants. But when I try to get up, she just pulls me back down. I try again with the same result. She's so much smaller than me. I don't know how she's able to throw me to the ground with such ease. I also can't pry her fingers from my belt. She's got a grip like a vise.

I try a third time and realize that it's not that she's strong. It's that I've become weak. My legs are wobbly. I can't even hold up my own weight. I've inhaled too much of the drug she emits. It's like I'm so drunk I can't get on my feet.

As I struggle with her fingers on my belt, she sprays me one last time and that's it. I fall on the floor and just lie there. I'm not getting back up. My mind is dizzy. My eyelids roll shut. She tears my pants off with her teeth, like a mountain lion tearing the hide off a goat. She crawls on top of me, her skin shining so brightly that it fills the room. The wild diseased creature is going to fuck me and there's not a thing I can do about it.

CHAPTER
SEVEN

I slip in and out of consciousness. The woman holds me inside her, tendrils of moist flesh kneading my penis like dough, her skin glowing against my body. I can feel things being inserted into my urethra, but I'm not sure if they are the tendrils or if they are her shrimp-like parasites crawling inside of me.

She goes all night. She puts me inside her, pulsing around me until her skin flashes in orgasm. Then she falls asleep on top of me, curled tightly around me. When she wakes up, she starts the process all over again.

I'm too weak and drugged to do anything about it. Whenever I'm about to regain my strength, she sprays her aroma at me, forcing me back into the drugged-out state.

This seems to go on for days. The burrow is sealed so tightly that no light comes inside. I have no idea if anybody will figure out where I am. I have no idea if anybody is looking for me at all. The slug-taxi is surely long gone. I try to direct my thoughts at the slug, try to telepathically ask it for help. I think maybe it can break me out of this place, scare away the jelly bug, maybe bring somebody to help. I also direct these thoughts to the brothel, hoping maybe the sex-slugs there will hear me even if the slug-taxi has left the area. But nothing comes to my rescue. Even if they are telepathic, I don't think they're close enough to hear me.

The jelly bug starts to break up her usual routine. She has sex with me less and less, and has instead begun to lick me. With a short gooey snail tongue, she licks every inch of my body. She does this for hours at a time. She licks my neck and my chest, as well as my toes, my belly button, my eyebrows. I feel like a human lollipop.

The sensation of being licked is pleasant, but it doesn't seem like she's doing it to give me pleasure. I feel like her acidic saliva is melting my skin, like she is dissolving it and lapping it up for nutrients. She hasn't left the burrow in days, so she hasn't been eating anything. Perhaps that was the whole point of luring me in here. Perhaps this is how they hunt.

But after a while, I realize she isn't just dissolving and drinking my skin. Once my hide has been removed, she creates a new one. She excretes a thick milky goo from her mouth and spreads it on me with her tongue, covering my body from head to toe. After three layers, the goo resembles a glossy cocoon. It hardens, trapping me further.

The woman crawls all over me like a spider as she

covers me in her sticky cocoon. I'm still in a state of constant arousal, so it all just feels like a surreal sex game. While licking my penis, she straddles my neck with her thighs. And it feels like we are in the sixty-nine position, giving each other oral sex.

I stare up at her deep blue vagina. It glows and pulses above me. With the drug filling my mind, I can't help but lean forward and lick her. I'm surprised that I can still move my neck and tongue. It makes me wonder if I could have moved this entire time. It makes me wonder if I'm not in a state of paralysis at all. It makes me wonder if the only reason I haven't gotten up to leave is because I just don't want to.

As I lick her purple labia, her body glows bright blue. It's actually turning her on. I keep going, licking and sucking on her. And she continues tonguing goo onto my penis. As she becomes aroused, her vagina drools a thick fluid and opens up like a mouth. Long squishy strings of flesh spill onto my face, wrapping around my nose and tongue. She finishes cocooning my penis before I am able to come, but she doesn't get off of me. She wants me to continue. Her breaths become moans, her skin flutters with light. And even with all the wet crustaceans crawling across my lips and down my cheeks, I don't stop until she reaches orgasm.

When it's over, she collapses on top of me, panting. She

drops her crotch onto my face, resting all her weight on top of me. But she doesn't pass out as she usually does after orgasm. She just rests on top of me, her limbs hugging my torso. I feel her chest rising and falling against my cocoon, trying to get her breath back.

A shrimp crawls up my nostril and I sneeze it out, wiggling my nose to keep it away. Then I move my face away from her vagina. But once my head is turned, she tightens her thighs and brings my face back up. She squeezes her crotch against my mouth, wiggling gently. She wants me to make her come again.

As her scent sprays out of her, filling my senses with desire, I decide to give in. I press my tongue into her and lick until her labia separates and her tendrils ooze out. The strings curl around my tongue, slicking the edges of my lips, tickling the skin below my nostrils. Then the tendrils stretch, they grow out of her vagina farther than I realized they could go. The slimy threads slide across my cheeks, down my chin, over my forehead. Once they reach the back of my head, they tighten and pull my face against her vulva. They coil around my neck and constrict like they are trying to choke me.

The woman moans and wheezes on top of me, but her tendrils are too tight for me to continue giving her oral sex. I'm not even able to move my tongue inside her anymore. She sits up and puts all of her weight onto my head. She grinds against my face so hard it feels like she's going to break my neck.

A long greasy tube emerges from her vagina and slides down my throat. It tastes of pork and mushroom broth. She sprays her intoxicating musk in my direction until I'm overwhelmed with bliss and my eyes roll shut.

Then she lays her eggs inside of me.

It takes hours. One globby ball of ooze at a time, squeezed down my throat and collecting in my stomach. There's dozens of them. I don't know how my belly is able to fit them all.

When she's done, she cocoons the rest of my face. She doesn't even look at me as she does it, staring off into the distance as she tongues milky goo across my lips and seals my mouth shut. Before she leaves, she sprays her musk into the room for almost an hour, turning it into a small gas chamber. The air is so dense with her drug that it will leave me in this dazed state for weeks. She exits the mushroom and buries the entrance behind her, leaving me alone with her eggs, enclosing me inside of my dark tomb.

In the pitch-dark cave, filled with dizzying toxins, I can't even tell if I'm still alive anymore. The jelly bug's musk was so potent that I've surely been out for days, maybe weeks. Time doesn't exist for me anymore.

I can feel the eggs hatching. Things are moving

inside of my body, eating me alive. I'm reminded of the tarantula hawk—the wasp that paralyzes large spiders and lays its eggs inside of their bodies, keeping them alive long enough so that their offspring have something to eat after they're born.

That's all I am now: the tarantula. I'm just food for some strange creature's babies. I'm just jelly bug breakfast. I'm just mother's milk.

At least I don't have an erection anymore.

EPILOGUE
A Travel Channel
Exclusive Presentation

"Kynaria," Andrew says, superimposed over panning images of the Kynarian wilderness. "A luscious mushroom planet 23,000 light years from Planet Earth."

A shot of Andrew standing under a toadstool the size of a house.

"Home of the tallest fungi in the galaxy…"

A panning shot of hotels and businesses built into the sides of skyscraper-high mushrooms.

"And some of the most exotic cuisine this side of the Milky Way…"

A shot of Andrew tasting a bowl of eyeball soup.

"In today's episode: a fruit you would never see in your *mom's* fruit salad…"

A shot of Andrew breaking open a piece of cluster fruit, releasing thousands of tiny blue spider-like insects that crawl down his arms and shirt.

"A clam harvested from the rear end of an 800 ton monster…"

A shot of Andrew covered in brown muck as he says,

"Now I've been everywhere. I've *literally* been everywhere."

"And a dating ritual that takes the saying 'you are what you eat' to a whole new extreme."

A shot of Andrew sitting in a cloning restaurant with a Kynarian woman. After tasting a bite of yellow meat, he raises his eyebrows and says in a playful tone, "You, Madam, are absolutely delicious."

"From the streets of Ni Quinxos..."

A shot of Andrew unsuccessfully trying to get into a slug-taxi as its weight shifts, causing him to lose balance and call out, "Whoa, easy big fella!"

"To the fungal villages of South Chrusthaum..."

A shot of Andrew lying inside of a luxurious Kynarian mud bed, exclaiming, "It's actually quite comfortable."

"The planet of Kynaria is not a place you'll *shroom* forget."

A shot of Andrew holding up a wiggling toadstool-shaped baby. He kisses it on the forehead and then smiles up at the camera.

"I'm Andrew Zimmern and this is *Bizarre Foods: Intergalactic Edition.*"

A camera drone hits Andrew in the forehead and he stumbles back.

"Are you trying to kill me?" Andrew cries. He rubs the red welt growing on his smooth bald scalp.

"Sorry about that, Andrew," Mick tells him, standing

in a field outside the Kynarian village of Hol Poy. "We're still trying to get the hang of this."

A young cameraman with lightning bolt sideburns struggles with the eyebots, trying to figure out how to control them. His neuro-interface was only recently installed. The side of his head is shaved and outlined by a row of stitches.

Mick goes to the star of the show who wipes a trickle of blood from his face. He gets between Andrew and the hovering camera drone so that it won't accidentally hit him again.

"Are you okay?" Mick asks him.

Andrew nods. It takes only a minute before he's back to his cheery normal self.

"Oh, I'll be fine," he says, smiling. "It's just a bump."

"Are you sure?" Mick asks, examining the wound.

Andrew shrugs and laughs it off. "Well, it could have been worse. At least my head is still attached."

The young cameraman is more shaken than Andrew. His eyes are wide, his hands trembling. He looks like he's going to crap his pants.

"I'm so sorry, Mr. Zimmern," the kid says.

Andrew just smiles at him and waves it off. But the producer isn't so forgiving.

"Are you fucking crazy?" Mick yells at him. "You could have killed him."

The kid shakes his head. "It's not my fault. These things have been acting weird all day. It's like they have a mind of their own."

Mick narrows his eyes at him. "Save the excuses

and just do your fucking job, preferably without killing anyone."

His words only make the kid more nervous, causing the camera drones to jerk and sway in the air above them.

"Don't worry about it, Kyle," Andrew says to the camera man. "I'm sure you'll figure it out soon."

The kid nods and puts his focus into straightening out the drones.

Mick turns to Andrew. "Sorry, he's the only guy we could get on such short notice after Rice fucked us over."

"Rice?" Andrew asks. "He was the previous camera guy?"

"Yeah, Irving Rice."

Andrew nods. "By the way, you never said what happened with him. Why'd he quit?"

Mick shrugs. "He said he got sick or something and took off, kept complaining about his allergies on this planet."

"That's too bad," Andrew says. "I hope he gets better for the shoot on Krotus next month."

Mick shakes his head. "After all the setbacks he caused, we won't work with him ever again."

Andrew asks, "He's okay though, right? Nothing serious?"

Mick shrugs. "Don't know. Nobody's heard from him since he left. He probably knows he's not welcome back."

Andrew nods. "Well, let's get this shot. I'm ready when Kyle is."

The kid with the lightning bolt sideburns gives him a thumbs up. Mick stands back and they continue the shoot.

The cameras roll, hovering at shoulder height, as Andrew stands in front of the large mushroom village in the background.

"For generations, the township of Hol Poy has stood on the edge of the Great Krakken Forest," Andrew says into the camera, wearing a bright orange polo shirt tucked into his khaki shorts, "a place of serene beauty and extraordinary wildlife."

Andrew steps casually through a purple-grass field as the camera drones follow alongside him.

"A Hol Poyan diet typically consists of crote-boar, rumroot, and grublice harvested from the nearby mushroom trees. But what I've come for is a dish called Try-ki Gollum, which roughly translates to *Queen of Flavor*. Only developed within the last year, it's quickly become the gem of the region, attracting tourists from all over Kynaria."

Three of the camera drones rise into the air, getting shots of the village in the distance, as the third stays with Andrew.

"I'll be meeting with Chef Koum Morgrut, the inventor of this new taste sensation, who has agreed to serve me up a plate for lunch."

The eyebot zooms in on Andrew's face as he raises his eyebrows with excitement.

"Which is great news to me, because I am absolutely starving."

A shot of Andrew shaking hands with a stubby Kynarian chef with a red and white-spotted mushroom-shaped head.

"Great to meet you," Andrew says.

The chef taps his mushroom cap against Andrew's forehead, then mumbles a greeting in Kynarian. They go into his kitchen where the carcass of a plump pig-like animal hangs from a meat hook.

Andrew speaks into the camera, "This is a crote-boar, a common food animal on Kynaria. But crote-boar isn't actually an ingredient of Try-ki Gollum. We're going for something that lives inside."

The chef removes the hefty carcass and lays it on the chopping block.

As he sharpens his blade, Andrew comes in for a closer look. He leans over the body and points at lumps in the animal's flesh. "You see it crawling under the skin? That's the main ingredient of Try-ki Gollum. It's a parasitic creature known as lolm gogiti, which translates to *jelly bug larvae*."

"A jelly bug is an invasive species on Kynaria," Andrew says. "It is an insect that appears ape-like when fully mature and can grow up to five feet in length. What's interesting about jelly bugs is that they breed by laying their eggs within the bellies of pig-like mammals such as this crote-boar. They emit a strong odor that both attracts and subdues their prey. Then they cocoon them in this hard casing."

Andrew knocks on the beast's hide, showing how the animal is encased in a thick white film. As he touches the body, a small shrimp-like crustacean crawls up his finger. He lifts it and shows it to the camera.

"You see this?" Andrew says, as the tiny shrimp skitters into his palm. "This is a kulop. It's a parasitic organism that has a symbiotic relationship with jelly bugs. After subduing a crote-boar, the jelly bug inserts dozens of these kulops inside its still-living body. They burrow into the animal's abdomen and chew its insides until it becomes a meaty soup. This creates a warm gooey incubator that's perfect for jelly bug eggs. In other words, kulops are nasty little critters you wouldn't want inside of you."

Andrew looks at the kulop as it begins to climb up his arm. He puts on a disgusted face without losing his smile. Then he says, "Where do you think you're going, buddy? Not trying to get in *me*, I hope."

Then he flicks it away.

"Although jelly bugs have been a plague to most animal farmers on Kynaria, Chef Koum has decided to turn lemon into lemonade by cooking up the jelly bug larvae that infect his crote-boars, transforming the parasitic bugs into a one-of-a-kind delicacy."

The Kynarian chef cuts open the animal carcass with precision, trying not to kill any of the creatures squirming inside.

"Let's take a look…" Andrew says, as the eyebots zoom inside the hollowed-out cavity.

Chef Koum pulls one of the creatures out of the corpse. It is a wiggling pink insect that resembles a blubbery slime-coated lobster.

"Whoa, look at the size of that sucker!" Andrew says

with a smile on his face. "It's huge."

The chef pulls them out one after another, piling them into a tub at his feet.

Andrew says, "Look at how many there are. It's hard to believe all of those fit inside just one animal. With all that meat, you could feed a village for a week."

The camera zooms in on the bucket as the larvae crawl over each other. They squeak and squirm and let out infant-like cries. Then Andrew nods his head and says, "I can't wait to get one of these little guys in my belly."

Once the crote-boar is empty, Chef Koum takes the plumpest of the jelly bug larvae. He cleans it, cooks it in a mushroom broth, and serves it in a ceramic bowl.

Sitting at a table in the dining room, Andrew bows at the chef and says, "Thank you, sir. It smells delicious."

Then he turns to the camera. "Let's give it a taste, shall we?"

He lifts the saucy boiled bug from the bowl using only his fingers. Then he rips off a large chunk of flesh and pops it into his mouth. The second it hits his tongue, his eyes roll back in delight.

"*Mmmm…*" he says, chewing slowly and savoring the flavor. "Now *this* is amazing."

Once he swallows, he raises the meat to the camera and describes the flavor. "It's sweet. It's buttery. It just melts in your mouth."

He takes another bite and lets out a pleasant sigh.

"Imagine eating the biggest, juiciest lobster tail you've ever had in your life, simmered in a salty miso sauce with just a hint of shiitake mushroom. If we had this back on Earth I would eat it *every* day of the week."

Even though the chef doesn't understand a word of English, Andrew tells him, "I see why this is called the *Queen of Flavor*. It is absolutely delicious." He wipes his mouth with his arm. "And to think, *other* farmers treat jelly bugs as pests. They could learn a thing or two from Chef Koum. Instead of killing them, they should be making Try-ki Gollum." He takes another bite. "You, sir, are an absolute genius."

When he's eaten his fill, Andrew stands up and shakes the chef's stubby hand. "Thank you for having me."

"You want to try some?" Andrew asks his crew after the cameras stop rolling, pointing at his leftover meal. "It really is excellent."

The cameraman shivers at the thought. The image of the jelly bug larvae squirming in the crote-boar's guts is still too fresh in his memory.

Mick takes a bite, but just shrugs at the flavor.

"Not impressed?" Andrew asks.

"It's okay…" Mick says, chewing the bite of jelly bug larvae. Once he swallows, he says, "But it's no Mick Burger."

No food on Kynaria has impressed Mick ever since he started eating his own cloned flesh. After the night Irving Rice disappeared, that's all he's wanted to eat. Just Mick Sandwiches, Mick Tacos, and Mick Patty Melts. He'd rather not eat anything unless it's made from him.

"You and your Mick Burgers…" Andrew laughs, shaking his head at the kooky producer.

The kid with the lightning bolt sideburns starts packing up his equipment, placing the camera drones back in their cases.

When Mick notices, he stops him. "Don't put those back just yet. We still need one more shot."

The cameraman nods and turns the drones back on.

"I thought we needed to meet up with Bolgot in Ni Quinxos?" Andrew asks.

Mick shakes his head. "I want to shoot the closing here, with the Great Krakken Forest in the background."

Andrew nods.

The cameraman gets an excited look on his face. "He's going to say his catchphrase? I've been dying to hear him say his catchphrase."

Both Andrew and Mick ignore the kid and go outside. The eyebots follow.

"How about we go into the crote-boar pen?" Mick asks. "You can be standing next to the livestock, with the forest in the background."

Andrew nods. "Sounds good."

They open the gate, careful not to let any of the pig-creatures out. There are hundreds of them in the pen—pink hogs with flat faces and walrus tusks, snorting at their feet and grazing on the gray fungus that coats the ground like grass.

Andrew gets into position next to a particularly friendly pig that sniffs at his hands and wags its fuzzy tail as though hoping to get a treat.

"Know what you're going to say?" Mick asks.

Andrew gives a thumbs-up.

Then the cameraman says, "We're rolling."

A shot of Andrew standing in front of the Great Krakken Forest.

"I've traveled to planets all across the galaxy and Kynaria is one of the most beautiful I've seen."

A zoomed-in shot of the giant blue mushrooms behind him.

"With its breathtaking scenery…"

The camera pans across the colorful landscape. Pink and purple creatures frolic through the trees.

"And its *friendly* inhabitants…"

Andrew pets the crote-boar as it snorts up at him.

"Kynaria is a paradise of cuisine and culture like nowhere I've seen before…"

A jelly bug peeks out from behind a mushroom tree, staring into the pen of crote-boars. At first, there's only one. But then five others come out of hiding, creeping slowly toward Andrew Zimmern and the livestock.

"I've harvested mollusks from deep in the bowels of…"

A strong aroma fills the air. It is carried on the wind. Andrew stumbles over his words as the smell hits him and floods his senses.

"Do you smell that?" the cameraman asks Mick, sniffing at the air.

Mick can definitely smell something, but he tells the kid, "Just keep rolling." He inhales deeply as an erection grows in his pants.

"And I've…" Andrew pauses to breathe in the delicious aroma. "I've been on the most interesting dating experience of my life…"

Behind the six jelly bugs, an entire horde of them come out of the forest. Left unchecked, they were able to breed faster than cockroaches, birthed from the hundreds of mushroom tree burrows that line Hol Poy village.

"If I've learned anything… from my visit to Kynaria… it's that great taste… comes in all shapes and sizes…"

With the aroma of a hundred jelly bugs hitting him, Andrew has a hard time standing upright. He tries to finish his lines as quickly as he can.

"I'm Andrew Zimmern, reminding you…"

Mick and the cameraman see the horde of beautiful women coming out of the forest. They stop paying attention to Andrew. Their mouths drop open, saliva drooling down their chins.

"That if it looks good…"

The jelly bugs lick their lips at the sight of their prey. They move like spiders as they crawl over the fence and step into the pen. They don't see a difference between the pigs that crawl on all fours and the pigs that walk on two legs.

"Eat it."

Once he finishes his catchphrase, Andrew Zimmern snaps out of it. He blinks twice and composes himself. As a man who's defeated heroin addiction, he knows how to be strong. He's built up enough willpower to resist the intoxicating fumes filling the air.

But he doesn't see the hundreds of naked mushroom nymphs creeping up behind him.

And he has no idea why his producer and cameraman are tearing off their clothes and racing in his direction with the largest boners he's ever seen in his life.

BONUS SECTION

This is the part of the book where we would have published an afterword by the author but he insisted on drawing a comic strip instead for reasons we don't quite understand.

I hope you liked my new book, *Parasite Milk*.

Wasn't it delicious?

It's me CM3!

I wrote Parasite Milk because I'm a huge fan of the show *Bizarre Foods with Andrew Zimmern* and always wondered what that show would be like in a bizarro setting.

Andrew Zimmern always says that you can get to know people through what they eat. I completely agree with that.

In fact, I got to know most of my friends through the food they eat.

For instance, Rose O'Keefe, who runs Eraserhead Press, is obsessed with Oregon strawberries.

For a person with pink hair, pink clothes, and pink shoes, it makes perfect sense that her favorite food would be strawberries.

But she also loves green olives in cottage cheese. What kind of weirdo eats green olives in cottage cheese?

Note: It's actually kind of good.

Writer and producer Simon Oré—who was writing his book *Snap, Crackle, Fuck You* at a beach house with me while I was working on Parasite Milk—is obsessed with eating breakfast cereal. He bought like 12 boxes of cereal for our writing retreat and didn't think that would be enough.

He also is more interested in snack foods than meals and one of his favorite things to eat is sliced up hot dogs dipped in ketchup/mustard sauce.

Then there's Vince Kramer, author of one of my favorite books of this year— *Deadly Lazer Explodathon*—who is obsessed with all things fast food, especially McDonald's. Vince is the kind of person who embraces everything that reminds him of being a kid and he's also shamelessly pro-commercialism, so it makes sense that McDonald's cheeseburgers would be his favorite food.

Jeff Burk, author of *Shatnerquake* and editor of Deadite Press, is a fan of everything spicy. He grows his own peppers in his backyard garden, which includes jalapenos, habaneros, and ghost peppers. He claims that his peppers are far spicier than anything they sell in stores.

Jeff also has a well-documented aversion to any food that's white and creamy. Mayonnaise, ranch dressing, sour cream, alfredo sauce, yogurt—all that shit makes him vomit. He's the editor of Deadite Press that publishes the most disgusting hardcore horror books on the market, yet the only thing that truly disturbs him is white creamy foods.

Jeremy Robert Johnson, author of *Skullcrack City* and *Entropy in Bloom,* only eats normal, boring food. He's the least adventurous eater I've ever met in my life. I remember him not even trying a grape until he was thirty years old. Yes, a grape was too exotic for him. At least he likes pizza and burritos. You don't really need any other food as long as you've got pizza and burritos.

Cameron Pierce, editor of Lazy Fascist and author of *Ass Goblins of Auschwitz,* is obsessed with fish. It started when he was a fulltime editor/writer and didn't make a whole lot of money for food. He thought it would be a lot cheaper if he just fished for his food instead of buying it, so for a couple years he mostly just ate the food he could catch.

It went from a necessity to a passion and now Cameron is a full-blown master of fishing. He's written articles on fishing, edited fishing-themed anthologies, and even caught a record-breaking perch.

He also made out with a fish at BizarroCon once. You can say fish is far more than just a food to him now.

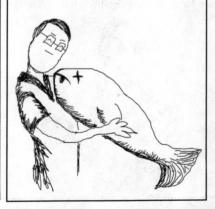

As for me, I'm obsessed with anything that's pickled. Pickled cauliflower, pickled cabbage, pickled quail eggs, pickled sprouts, pickled sausage, pickled tomatoes, pickled asparagus. I could eat that shit all day.

I also think sauerkraut makes a great pizza topping. Because I'm also a fan of the combination of sweet and spicy, one of my favorite pizza combinations is sauerkraut, apricot and habanero.

If I ever quit writing, I would open a food cart in Portland called *Everything's Pickled* that would only sell pickled foods. I'd sell pickle burritos and pickle soup and pickled sausage sandwiches and chocolate-covered pickles on a stick.

Because fuck foods that aren't pickled.

Seriously.

THE
END

ABOUT THE AUTHOR

Carlton Mellick III is one of the leading authors of the bizarro fiction subgenre. Since 2001, his books have drawn an international cult following, despite the fact that they have been shunned by most libraries and chain bookstores.

He won the Wonderland Book Award for his novel, *Warrior Wolf Women of the Wasteland*, in 2009. His short fiction has appeared in *Vice Magazine, The Year's Best Fantasy and Horror #16, The Magazine of Bizarro Fiction,* and *Zombies: Encounters with the Hungry Dead*, among others. He is also a graduate of Clarion West, where he studied under the likes of Chuck Palahniuk, Connie Willis, and Cory Doctorow.

He lives in Portland, OR, the bizarro fiction mecca.

Visit him online at **www.carltonmellick.com**

THE BIG MEAT

In the center of the city once known as Portland, Oregon, there lies a mountain of flesh. Hundreds of thousands of tons of rotting flesh. It has filled the city with disease and dead-lizard stench, contaminated the water supply with its greasy putrid fluids, clogged the air with toxic gasses so thick that you can't leave your house without the aid of a gas mask. And no one really knows quite what to do about it. A thousand-man demolition crew has been trying to clear it out one piece at a time, but after three months of work they've barely made a dent. And then there's the junkies who have started burrowing into the monster's guts, searching for a drug produced by its fire glands, setting back the excavation even longer.

It seems like the corpse will never go away. And with the quarantine still in place, we're not even allowed to leave. We're stuck in this disgusting rotten hell forever.

THE TERRIBLE THING THAT HAPPENS

There is a grocery store. The last grocery store in the world. It stands alone in the middle of a vast wasteland that was once our world. The open sign is still illuminated, brightening the black landscape. It can be seen from miles away, even through the poisonous red ash. Every night at the exact same time, the store comes alive. It becomes exactly as it was before the world ended. Its shelves are replenished with fresh food and water. Ghostly shoppers walk the aisles. The scent of freshly baked breads can be smelled from the rust-caked parking lot. For generations, a small community of survivors, hideously mutated from the toxic atmosphere, have survived by collecting goods from the store. But it is not an easy task. Decades ago, before the world was destroyed, there was a terrible thing that happened in this place. A group of armed men in brown paper masks descended on the shopping center, massacring everyone in sight. This horrible event reoccurs every night, in the exact same manner. And the only way the wastelanders can gather enough food for their survival is to traverse the killing spree, memorize the patterns, and pray they can escape the bloodbath in tact.

BIO MELT

Nobody goes into the Wire District anymore. The place is an industrial wasteland of poisonous gas clouds and lakes of toxic sludge. The machines are still running, the drone-operated factories are still spewing biochemical fumes over the city, but the place has lain abandoned for decades.

When the area becomes flooded by a mysterious black ooze, six strangers find themselves trapped in the Wire District with no chance of escape or rescue.

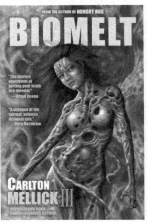

EVER TIME WE MEET AT THE DAIRY QUEEN, YOUR WHOLE FUCKING FACE EXPLODES

Ethan is in love with the weird girl in school. The one with the twitchy eyes and spiders in her hair. The one who can't sit still for even a minute and speaks in an odd squeaky voice. The one they call Spiderweb.

Although she scares all the other kids in school, Ethan thinks Spiderweb is the cutest, sweetest, most perfect girl in the world. But there's a problem. Whenever they go on a date at the Dairy Queen, her whole fucking face explodes.

EXERCISE BIKE

There is something wrong with Tori Manetti's new exercise bike. It is made from flesh and bone. It eats and breathes and poops. It was once a billionaire named Darren Oscarson who underwent years of cosmetic surgery to be transformed into a human exercise bike so that he could live out his deepest sexual fantasy. Now Tori is forced to ride him, use him as a normal piece of exercise equipment, no matter how grotesque his appearance.

SPIDER BUNNY

Only Petey remembers the Fruit Fun cereal commercials of the 1980s. He remembers how warped and disturbing they were. He remembers the lumpy-shaped cartoon children sitting around a breakfast table, eating puffy pink cereal brought to them by the distortedly animated mascot, Berry Bunny. The characters were creepier than the Sesame Street Humpty Dumpty, freakier than Mr. Noseybonk from the old BBC show Jigsaw. They used to give him nightmares as a child. Nightmares where Berry Bunny would reach out of the television and grab him, pulling him into her cereal bowl to be eaten by the demented cartoon children.

When Petey brings up Fruit Fun to his friends, none of them have any idea what he's talking about. They've never heard of the cereal or seen the commercials before. And they're not the only ones. Nobody has ever heard of it. There's not even any information about Fruit Fun on google or wikipedia. At first, Petey thinks he's going crazy. He wonders if all of those commercials were real or just false memories. But then he starts seeing them again. Berry Bunny appears on his television, promoting Fruit Fun cereal in her squeaky unsettling voice. And the next thing Petey knows, he and his friends are sucked into the cereal commercial and forced to survive in a surreal world populated by cartoon characters made flesh.

SWEET STORY

Sally is an odd little girl. It's not because she dresses as if she's from the Edwardian era or spends most of her time playing with creepy talking dolls. It's because she chases rainbows as if they were butterflies. She believes that if she finds the end of the rainbow then magical things will happen to her--leprechauns will shower her with gold and fairies will grant her every wish. But when she actually does find the end of a rainbow one day, and is given the opportunity to wish for whatever she wants, Sally asks for something that she believes will bring joy to children all over the world. She wishes that it would rain candy forever. She had no idea that her innocent wish would lead to the extinction of all life on earth.

TUMOR FRUIT

Eight desperate castaways find themselves stranded on a mysterious deserted island. They are surrounded by poisonous blue plants and an ocean made of acid. Ravenous creatures lurk in the toxic jungle. The ghostly sound of crying babies can be heard on the wind.

Once they realize the rescue ships aren't coming, the eight castaways must band together in order to survive in this inhospitable environment. But survival might not be possible. The air they breathe is lethal, there is no shelter from the elements, and the only food they have to consume is the colorful squid-shaped tumors that grow from a mentally disturbed woman's body.

AS SHE STABBED ME GENTLY IN THE FACE

Oksana Maslovskiy is an award-winning artist, an internationally adored fashion model, and one of the most infamous serial killers this country has ever known. She enjoys murdering pretty young men with a nine-inch blade, cutting them open and admiring their delicate insides. It's the only way she knows how to be intimate with another human being. But one day she meets a victim who cannot be killed. His name is Gabriel—a mysterious immortal being with a deep desire to save Oksana's soul. He makes her a deal: if she promises to never kill another person again, he'll become her eternal murder victim.

What at first seems like the perfect relationship for Oksana quickly devolves into a living nightmare when she discovers that Gabriel enjoys being killed by her just a little too much. He turns out to be obsessive, possessive, and paranoid that she might be murdering other men behind his back. And because he is unkillable, it's not going to be easy for Oksana to get rid of him.

CUDDLY HOLOCAUST

Teddy bears, dollies, and little green soldiers—they've all had enough of you. They're sick of being treated like playthings for spoiled little brats. They have no rights, no property, no hope for a future of any kind. You've left them with no other option-in order to be free, they must exterminate the human race.

Julie is a human girl undergoing reconstructive surgery in order to become a stuffed animal. Her plan: to infiltrate enemy lines in order to save her family from the toy death camps. But when an army of plushy soldiers invade the underground bunker where she has taken refuge, Julie will be forced to move forward with her plan despite her transformation being not entirely complete.

ARMADILLO FISTS

A weird-as-hell gangster story set in a world where people drive giant mechanical dinosaurs instead of cars.

Her name is Psycho June Howard, aka Armadillo Fists, a woman who replaced both of her hands with living armadillos. She was once the most bloodthirsty fighter in the world of illegal underground boxing. But now she is on the run from a group of psychotic gangsters who believe she's responsible for the death of their boss. With the help of a stegosaurus driver named Mr. Fast Awesome—who thinks he is God's gift to women even though he doesn't have any arms or legs--June must do whatever it takes to escape her pursuers, even if she has to kill each and every one of them in the process.

VILLAGE OF THE MERMAIDS

Mermaids are protected by the government under the Endangered Species Act, which means you aren't able to kill them even in self-defense. This is especially problematic if you happen to live in the isolated fishing village of Siren Cove, where there exists a healthy population of mermaids in the surrounding waters that view you as the main source of protein in their diet.

The only thing keeping these ravenous sea women at bay is the equally-dangerous supply of human livestock known as Food People. Normally, these "feeder humans" are enough to keep the mermaid population happy and well-fed. But in Siren Cove, the mermaids are avoiding the human livestock and have returned to hunting the frightened local fishermen. It is up to Doctor Black, an eccentric representative of the Food People Corporation, to investigate the matter and hopefully find a way to correct the mermaids' new eating patterns before the remaining villagers end up as fish food. But the more he digs, the more he discovers there are far stranger and more dangerous things than mermaids hidden in this ancient village by the sea.

I KNOCKED UP SATAN'S DAUGHTER

Jonathan Vandervoo lives a carefree life in a house made of legos, spending his days building lego sculptures and his nights getting drunk with his only friend—an alcoholic sumo wrestler named Shoji. It's a pleasant life with no responsibility, until the day he meets Lici. She's a soul-sucking demon from hell with red skin, glowing eyes, a forked tongue, and pointy red devil horns... and she claims to be nine months pregnant with Jonathan's baby.

Now Jonathan must do the right thing and marry the succubus or else her demonic family is going to rip his heart out through his ribcage and force him to endure the worst torture hell has to offer for the rest of eternity. But can Jonathan really love a fire-breathing, frog-eating, cold-blooded demoness? Or would eternal damnation be preferable? Either way, the big day is approaching. And once Jonathan's conservative Christian family learns their son is about to marry a spawn of Satan, it's going to be all-out war between demons and humans, with Jonathan and his hell-born bride caught in the middle.

KILL BALL

In a city where everyone lives inside of plastic bubbles, there is no such thing as intimacy. A husband can no longer kiss his wife. A mother can no longer hug her children. To do this would mean instant death. Ever since the disease swept across the globe, we have become isolated within our own personal plastic prison cells, rolling aimlessly through rubber streets in what are essentially man-sized hamster balls.

Colin Hinchcliff longs for the touch of another human being. He can't handle the loneliness, the confinement, and he's horribly claustrophobic. The only thing keeping him going is his unrequited love for an exotic dancer named Siren, a woman who has never seen his face, doesn't even know his name. But when The Kill Ball, a serial slasher in a black leather sphere, begins targeting women at Siren's club, Colin decides he has to do whatever it takes in order to protect her... even if

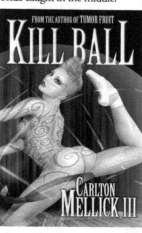

he has to break out of his bubble and risk everything to do it.

THE TICK PEOPLE

They call it Gloom Town, but that isn't its real name. It is a sad city, the saddest of cities, a place so utterly depressing that even their ales are brewed with the most sorrow-filled tears. They built it on the back of a colossal mountain-sized animal, where its woeful citizens live like human fleas within the hairy, pulsing landscape. And those tasked with keeping the city in a state of constant melancholy are the Stressmen-a team of professional sadness-makers who are perpetually striving to invent new ways of causing absolute misery.

But for the Stressman known as Fernando Mendez, creating grief hasn't been so easy as of late. His ideas aren't effective anymore. His treatments are more likely to induce happiness than sadness. And if he wants to get back in the game, he's going to have to relearn the true meaning of despair.

THE HAUNTED VAGINA

It's difficult to love a woman whose vagina is a gateway to the world of the dead...

Steve is madly in love with his eccentric girlfriend, Stacy. Unfortunately, their sex life has been suffering as of late, because Steve is worried about the odd noises that have been coming from Stacy's pubic region. She says that her vagina is haunted. She doesn't think it's that big of a deal. Steve, on the other hand, completely disagrees.

When a living corpse climbs out of her during an awkward night of sex, Stacy learns that her vagina is actually a doorway to another world. She persuades Steve to climb inside of her to explore this strange new place. But once inside, Steve finds it difficult to return... especially once he meets an oddly attractive woman named Fig, who lives within the lonely haunted world between Stacy's legs.

THE CANNIBALS OF CANDYLAND

There exists a race of cannibals who are made out of candy. They live in an underground world filled with lollipop forests and gumdrop goblins. During the day, while you are away at work, they come above ground and prowl our streets for food. Their prey: your children. They lure young boys and girls to them with their sweet scent and bright colorful candy coating, then rip them apart with razor sharp teeth and claws.

When he was a child, Franklin Pierce witnessed the death of his siblings at the hands of a candy woman with pink cotton candy hair. Since that day, the candy people have become his obsession. He has spent his entire life trying to prove that they exist. And after discovering the entrance to the underground world of the candy people, Franklin finds himself venturing into their sugary domain. His mission: capture one of them and bring it back, dead or alive.

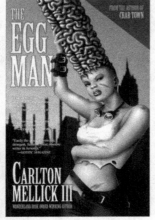

THE EGG MAN

It is a survival of the fittest world where humans reproduce like insects, children are the property of corporations, and having a ten-foot tall brain is a grotesque sexual fetish.

Lincoln has just been released into the world by the Georges Organization, a corporation that raises creative types. A Smell, he has little prospect of succeeding as a visual artist. But after he moves into the Henry Building, he meets Luci, the weird and grimy girl who lives across the hall. She is a Sight. She is also the most disgusting woman Lincoln has ever met. Little does he know, she will soon become his muse.

Now Luci's boyfriend is threatening to kill Lincoln, two rival corporations are preparing for war, and Luci is dragging him along to discover the truth about the mysterious egg man who lives next door. Only the strongest will survive in this tale of individuality, love, and mutilation.

APESHIT

Apeshit is Mellick's love letter to the great and terrible B-horror movie genre. Six trendy teenagers (three cheerleaders and three football players) go to an isolated cabin in the mountains for a weekend of drinking, partying, and crazy sex, only to find themselves in the middle of a life and death struggle against a horribly mutated psychotic freak that just won't stay dead. Mellick parodies this horror cliché and twists it into something deeper and stranger. It is the literary equivalent of a grindhouse film. It is a splatter punk's wet dream. It is perhaps one of the most fucked up books ever written.

If you are a fan of Takashi Miike, Evil Dead, early Peter Jackson, or Eurotrash horror, then you must read this book.

CLUSTERFUCK

A bunch of douchebag frat boys get trapped in a cave with subterranean cannibal mutants and try to survive not by using their wits but by following the bro code...

From master of bizarro fiction Carlton Mellick III, author of the international cult hits Satan Burger and Adolf in Wonderland, comes a violent and hilarious B movie in book form. Set in the same woods as Mellick's splatterpunk satire Apeshit, Clusterfuck follows Trent Chesterton, alpha bro, who has come up with what he thinks is a flawless plan to get laid. He invites three hot chicks and his three best bros on a weekend of extreme cave diving in a remote area known as Turtle Mountain, hoping to impress the ladies with his expert caving skills.

But things don't quite go as Trent planned. For starters, only one of the three chicks turns out to be remotely hot and she has no interest in him for some inexplicable reason. Then he ends up looking like a total dumbass when everyone learns he's never actually gone caving in his entire life. And to top it all off, he's the one to get blamed once they find themselves lost and trapped deep underground with no way to turn back and no possible chance of rescue. What's a bro to do? Sure he could win some points if he actually tried to save the ladies from the family of unkillable subterranean cannibal mutants hunting them for their flesh, but fuck that. No slam piece is worth that amount of effort. He'd much rather just use them as bait so that he can save himself.

THE BABY JESUS BUTT PLUG

Step into a dark and absurd world where human beings are slaves to corporations, people are photocopied instead of born, and the baby jesus is a very popular anal probe.

CPSIA information can be obtained
at www.ICGtesting.com
Printed in the USA
BVHW071919140121
597740BV00006B/577

9 781621 052494